THE FACE YOU WEAR

FAITH PIERCE

Let the world know:
#IGotMyCLPBook!

Crystal Lake Publishing
www.CrystalLakePub.com

WELCOME
TO ANOTHER

CRYSTAL LAKE PUBLISHING
CREATION

Join today at www.crystallakepub.com & www.patreon.com/CLP

PART ONE

CHAPTER ONE

WE HAD BEEN married only two weeks when it started. The soft creak of the bedroom door woke me and I sat up, enveloped in a sleepy trance. Michael's dark silhouette faced me. He stood in the doorway, outlined against the dim moonlight filtering into the hall. The clock at my side showed after four o'clock in the morning.

I parted my lips to speak.

What are you doing? It's so late, I wanted to say. We had talked about this, fought about it. He agreed that his schedule had been too unpredictable and that he'd change it. No more eating, sleeping, living at different times.

But the words piled up in my mouth, too much effort to make.

Speaking would push me further into wakefulness, chasing away any more sleep. Exhaustion weighed on me, and any movement except laying back down seemed impossible. Through heavy lids, I watched him move toward me as I fell back into a deep sleep.

That morning I stared at his sleeping form, wondering what kept him up so late, but I didn't say anything to him in our brief exchange before I went to work and left him curled in bed. It nagged at me though, all through the swirl of morning meetings and planning client assignments, hovering in the back of my mind while I worked.

Four o'clock in the morning. His saying one thing and doing the other, his disregard for my schedule, it prickled under my skin.

Not to mention that our black shepherd mix Holly was at her most energetic in the mornings, and she expected early walks since Michael worked from home. It didn't seem fair to change her routine from one day to the next for no reason.

I considered texting to ask what was going on, to confirm he'd taken Holly for her morning walk, and that he wasn't sleeping so late that he might miss important deadlines or meetings, but I held back. We had just gotten married, after all.

In my first days back at work after our honeymoon, everyone's usual greetings expanded. Now they included, *"So how's married life?"* and *"How's the husband?"* and *"How are you two settling in?"*

"It's all pretty much the same as couples-living-together life," I wanted to say, since we had lived together for more than a year, but I would smile back and say everything was great instead.

And I knew it wasn't the same, not really. Up until the very last minute before our wedding, I kept expecting it not to happen. With my family being what it was—an unstable mess—marriage had always seemed like a maybe for me; especially marriage to someone as normal and well-adjusted as Michael. It was the last puzzle piece clicking into place. And with it, something shifted: I felt a sense of belonging I'd never had before. I took the commitment seriously and tried my best to make it without illusion. We weren't perfect, but we were good. We were going to make it work. The doors out were barred; we willingly agreed to close them, together. That was how I thought of marriage, anyway.

***

"Jana, you should bring him to happy hour tonight," my boss Devin announced at the weekly department meeting.

"Oh, I don't know," I said, trying not to wince at the weak laugh that escaped my throat. *No one wants the mood dampened by the manager*, I wanted to say. But Devin was my boss and the director of the entire department, and he had a different perspective. His insistence on attending every happy hour was the only reason I found myself obligated to show up every now and then.

Never had I suspected when I chose a career path in forensic accounting that happy hours would be such a regular part of it, but most of my coworkers were as serious about their social drinking as they were about their annual reports.

He was the "cool boss" type, but effortlessly so. Like he couldn't be any other way if he tried. He had straight white teeth and a brilliant smile, and he wore tailored suits. He maintained a neatly trimmed five o'clock shadow that rose to a perfectly straight line halfway up his dark brown cheeks. Sometimes I found myself staring at his face, trying to decipher whether one side was a millimeter higher than the other. It never was.

"It's lucky we have a happy hour scheduled your first week back," he continued. "It'll be our welcome-to-the-team shindig for Maria slash congrats to you and Michael."

Maria, young and fresh from college, was sitting a few seats down and looked up eagerly at the sound of her name. Her short brown hair curled under her jawline and framed her heart-shaped face delightfully.

"Congratulations by the way, Jana," she said to me, smiling like nothing in the world could please her more than sharing her welcome happy hour with us. And maybe she really was glad to share the spotlight; I couldn't imagine anyone actually enjoying being the sole focus of a social event where they're still trying to figure out everyone's names.

"Thank you," I said, hoping my smile equaled hers in warmth.

"You can bring the new ball and chain, right?" Devin jumped back in, asking the question like he was asking whether I could handle a project or meet an important deadline.

"Sure," I said as calmly as I could muster.

"Great. That's great. We're all such workaholics around here, it's nice for spouses to get to meet the people you spend all your time with. Besides, you've been here what, a year?"

Eight months.

"And I don't think anyone on the team has met him."

"Well, you'll get to meet him now." I tried to feign excitement but inside dread filled me.

I messaged Michael as soon as I reached my desk after the meeting, and he agreed to come without hesitation. It didn't make much sense that he was the one who worked from home; he got as excited about social gatherings as Holly got about going on walks.

***

When we arrived at the bar that night, I knew immediately that Devin had chosen the place. It was the kind of bar that calls itself a lounge and has a special drinks menu solely for their dozens of different martinis. Devin bought the first round, gesturing with a subtle hand motion to let the server know it was on him. I noticed, but everyone else was distracted and chattering and didn't seem to see. I squirmed, wondering how I was supposed to handle it. Was I supposed to thank him right then, while still empty-handed? Or would that be presumptuous, since the motion could have meant something else? But what if he noticed me noticing and considered my silence rude? Surely no one buys drinks for two large tables of people without expecting to be acknowledged.

"Jana, how did you two meet?" Maria's voice broke my miserable reverie and I met her eyes, friendly but with a hint of something I thought might be desperation. In the time it took for our group to place a drink order, Maria had been welcomed to the team in typical fashion—an intense interrogation on everything from her pets and musical tastes to her college history and the cities where she had lived. I sympathized, but I was the last person with the social graces or the nerve to rescue her.

"We volunteered together," I said, but before she could ask where or offer any kind of reply, I asked her if she was seeing anyone.

"Oh, gosh, I guess it's a little complicated," she said with a short laugh. And it was, as complicated as I could have hoped from a recent graduate in a new city, touching on everything from an aversion to labels to an ill-advised long-distance attempt, and the conversation swelled forward without dwelling on me. The drinks came and I thanked Devin with everyone else, and tried to relax while I sipped my wine and hoped no one would call on me.

Michael, by contrast, interjected frequently and didn't hesitate to answer questions about his family, job, hobbies, or anything else that came up. Within half an hour, the table knew he worked freelance doing the kind of technical work that most people could hear explained twice and then still repeat as, "Something with computers I think," if they were asked what he did. They knew about his passion for free educational tools for kids and that he volunteered his time doing online tutoring, and about our dog, and his family and his hometown.

Meanwhile, I sat with a knot pressing against my gut and tried to remember it was normal for them to know these things, and that there was nothing wrong with that. That this little piece of my life wouldn't give anything away.

At some point he mentioned my sister Ivy's bookshop and told everyone they needed to go see it.

"It's not a normal bookshop," he said. "It's got this really cool outdoor section, like a shared patio with a coffee shop downtown. You can sit outside and read while you have coffee, snacks, whatever. It's a nice spot."

I was flooded with warmth at this unexpected praise of my

sister's business, and gave him an appreciative smile when he turned and caught my eye.

By the time I finished my second glass of wine nearly an hour later, sipping carefully because the last thing I could stomach was the thought of having to face these people in the morning after a night of loosened inhibitions, most of my coworkers were at least a drink ahead of me and laughter was ringing out freely and often.

At one point, Maria made the mistake of mentioning the service she was being trained on, and Devin slapped his palm on the table and admonished her, "No more work talk!"

Several people cheered and raised their glasses and Maria laughed, and I realized I couldn't say how long a smile had been spread across my face.

Still, by the time another hour had passed and another glass of wine with it, I was ready to end the social experiment. I pressed Michael's hand under the table, hoping he'd understand, but it took a subtle text message before he got the hint.

"All right, we'd better be off," he finally said, to my relief. "I've got some work to do in the morning."

Since he could do his work any time of day, I knew he was making that up for me, and I wanted to hug him. We said our goodbyes and went out to the parking lot, where he grabbed my wrist and pulled me into his chest. He thought nothing of public displays of affection, but I did a quick scan to make sure none of my coworkers were making their departures behind us before leaning into him.

"That wasn't so terrible, was it?" he asked. "They seem nice."

"You're right," I said. The evening had drained me and I couldn't wait to be home, but I had to admit to myself that it hadn't been as bad as I had expected. I even felt a pang of remorse over how uninterested I'd been in getting to know my coworkers. "I guess I should get out of my comfort zone more often. It's easier when I'm with you."

"I'm glad," he said, and I kissed his cheek.

"Hey," I said abruptly, the wine dulling my restraint just enough, "Why'd you come to bed so late last night?"

"What?" He paused, standing in the dimly lit parking lot, keys dangling from his hand, and looked at me blankly.

"You came to bed after four a.m. Don't you remember? It woke me up. I'm surprised I was able to go back to sleep at all before I had to get up for work."

He rubbed his neck and glanced toward his car. "Jana, I came to bed an hour after you last night. It was around midnight."

I was sure he was confused. "Not last night," I said.

"Yes, last night. And I haven't stayed up later than two all week."

My earlier irritation with him was being pulled out from under me, and I cast my mind back to the figure in the doorway, moving toward me, now ominous and dark. I looked around the half-empty parking lot and shivered.

I stood in silence, not knowing how to explain the figure I saw.

"Did you have a dream or something?" he asked over his shoulder, already moving toward the car and opening the door.

"I guess. Nothing major. I thought I woke up and you were standing in the doorway. I sat up and looked at the clock and it was after four. And I went back to sleep before anything else happened. It felt so real."

I wondered if it could have been someone else in our home, but that didn't seem likely. It had to have been a dream.

Michael stood next to his open door, arm draped over it, and shrugged. "That's weird. You must be looking for reasons to be annoyed with me."

I laughed. "Like I need to look." I pushed the image of the dark figure approaching our bed out of my mind, and leaned over to kiss him.

When I began to pull away, he caught my arm and stopped me, dragging me against him and wrapping me in a hug. He nuzzled his nose against my neck and rested his face there. I let him tuck me against him, in spite of the public location and my coworkers' possible appearances. The exchange was already forgotten for him.

If the dreams had stopped there, I probably would have forgotten it, too.

CHAPTER TWO

"**J**AAAANA!" **IVY'S VOICE** rang through the house as she came through the front door, and Holly sprang from her position sprawled on the kitchen floor where she'd been alternating between dozing and watching me and Michael work.

"Oh, she's early. Sorry, do you have this?" I let go of the cabinet door I'd been holding steady while Michael unscrewed it.

"Jeez, sure," he said, grabbing the bottom of the door. "No thanks to you," he called after me as I darted from the kitchen.

I grinned over my shoulder. "I knew you had it."

"Sure you did. Or you no longer care about my safety since we're married. All part of your plot to get the insurance money."

"Right. Death by stubbed toe."

I met Ivy halfway through our living room, Holly prancing around her in excitement.

"Sounds serious," she said, and threw her arms around me. We had seen each other briefly right after we got back from our honeymoon because she kept Holly for us, but it had been a couple weeks since then and it was unusual for us to go that long without seeing each other.

"Jana!" She released me from her tight hug, but her hands lingered on my shoulders and she looked at my face. "Holy shit, you're married!" Her voice maintained soft traces of the Alabama twang that I had determinedly scrubbed from my own speech, and it was especially pronounced when she swore, which was often.

I laughed. "Yes, still."

She had greeted me that way the last time I saw her too, and she hadn't been able to stop saying it at our reception.

"All right, I'll quit," she said. "Hell, someday I might even be used to it."

"You might beat me to it." We walked back toward the kitchen where Michael was stacking the cabinet doors against the wall.

"Hi, Michael," Ivy said.

Michael said hi and greeted her with a hug. Ivy was the only person in my family I'd ever been regularly affectionate with, but Michael's entire family were huggers and it didn't matter if they were seeing each other for the second time in a single day.

"Big project?" she asked as he released her.

"Yeah, we've been wanting to do the cabinets since we moved in. Figured we might as well tackle it."

"Nice. What color?"

"White," he said. "We're boring."

"You said you wanted white," I said, staring at the gallon of paint I picked out earlier that day.

"Sure. I like boring." He smiled and wiped his hands on his jeans. "Well, I would definitely keep working on this all by myself while Jana takes a break to visit, but I'm sure you two want some peace and quiet in here so I'll just head upstairs for a bit."

"Oh, no," Ivy cut in. "It's a real nice day, Michael, pretty sure we'll be comfy on the porch if you want to keep working."

He was already out of the room and to the stairs. "I want you to have options!" he called behind him. "Have fun now, bye-bye."

Ivy snorted a laugh at his retreating figure. "Hope you weren't in a rush to get this done," she said to me.

"Not at all." I went to fetch glasses. "Tea, lemonade?"

"Sweet tea sounds good," she said.

"Did you want to go out to the porch?" I asked once our drinks were in hand.

"Nah, I was messing with him. It's humid as shit. We can stay here where it's cool and the snacks are nearby." We settled in to catch up, Ivy chattering and asking questions like we hadn't seen each other in months.

We have different fathers, and there was nothing at first glance to connect us. She was only a few years older than me, but Michael once told me it looked like a decade separated us. If I was objective and forgot my affection for a moment, I knew he was right. Ivy's teens and most of her twenties had been difficult years, much more so than mine since she had taken responsibility for our mother until the end. Now in her early thirties, fine lines gathered around her lips, and her eyes had a hardness I couldn't define.

Ivy's figure was full and soft where mine was thin and straight, and her skin was a few shades darker than mine. My hair hung lifeless to my shoulders while hers burst from her head in rich brown curls. She was wearing her usual bright colors that afternoon, a flowing cardigan of pink, green, and yellow flowers, contrasting sharply with my jeans and brown t-shirt. I could claim it was only because I'd been working on the house, but the truth was that I usually wore solids and neutral colors. I was impressed by Ivy's style, but never daring enough to emulate it. Multiple rings adorned her fingers and with every movement to bring the glass of tea to her lips, bracelets jingled at the end of an arm wrapped in intricate, winding tattoos. The only jewelry I wore was my wedding set and small studs in my ears. And yet, sitting comfortably with her as I did so often, I would have been surprised if even a stranger needed to be told we were sisters.

Ivy was catching me up on her living situation. She hadn't had any luck finding a new apartment; her current lease was less than two months from expiring, and she hated her landlord.

"You could probably use our guest room until you find someplace," I said.

"Nah, that's okay. I hate moving so damn much that if I went through the effort of getting here, I'd never want to leave again. How do you think I ended up staying so long in my current shithole?"

"Fair enough. Maybe I can help you look this weekend. And if it doesn't work out, the offer still stands."

"I appreciate that. But y'all need your space. I'm sure I'll find something. Besides, you never know when you might need to get that room ready for your own purposes." She arched her eyebrows and grinned.

I forced a smile. "I don't know about that."

"I know y'all aren't in any rush," she said. "But you never know."

"Sure. I think Michael's pretty much ready when I am. He can't wait to be a dad." I tried not to sound as unsure as I felt, but I felt Ivy's eyes on my face even while I kept my gaze on the window, focused on a squirrel that hovered on the porch rail.

"You sound iffy." She was never one to beat around the bush. "Are you wanting to wait, or are you on the fence about kids entirely?"

"Oh, no," I hurried to reassure her. I nervously looked around as though Michael could hear us, even though I knew he was upstairs. "I want to, eventually."

We sat in silence for a moment and I tried to think of a way to change the subject, my mind running through a list of topics we'd already covered, but my anxiety was permeating the air like a mist and I knew Ivy was picking up on it.

"What are you worried about?" she asked before I could think of a way to avoid it. "Is it because of Mom?"

I almost dropped my mug, never used to the way she could casually broach any subject no matter how dark or painful, without a thought, and it took all my restraint not to glance behind me to make sure Michael hadn't come down without me hearing him.

"No," I said, trying to sound as calm as she did and hoping she couldn't tell how uncomfortable the topic made me. "I mean, I don't know. Maybe."

"Well, what does Michael think about it?"

He doesn't know.

"He's fine with it," I lied. "He thinks it'll be fine. I'm sure he's right. Anyway, like you said, there's no rush." I had always meant to tell him, never meant for things to get so far without him knowing. My chest tightened, but I managed to smile at Ivy.

"Sure." Her gaze stayed steady on my face as silence fell again and I knew she wanted to push, wanted to reassure me or ask more questions about why I was being so odd about it. I got up and walked around the counter to get more lemonade, even though my glass was still half-full.

"Do you need more tea?" I asked, pretending not to see that hers was full.

"No," she said. "You know, there are options if you're worried . . . "

"Ivy," I snapped, unable to take it anymore. "I have enough on my hands right now. It's not something I'm worried about yet." I gave an exasperated laugh to cover my shortness and forced lightness back into my voice. "We just got married. Lord. Calm your tits." It was a phrase Ivy used often and I stole it then, knowing it would make her laugh to hear me saying it. I couldn't imagine saying it to anyone else in the world.

She laughed out loud with her head thrown back, like I knew she would. "Excuse me! Calm your own damn tits, thank you very much. But fine. I know there's no rush. Let me know if you ever need to talk about it, kay?"

"I will," I said, knowing I would not.

***

Ivy didn't stay for much more than an hour; Michael and I tackled the cabinets with renewed energy and were able to get them removed, sanded, and primed on one side. We ordered takeout for dinner and Michael opened a bottle of wine to go with it.

By the time I was ready for bed, I was light-headed and buzzing with pleasant warmth. I snuck up behind Michael while he put away the last of the dishes, careful to sidestep Holly where she curled up on the rug in front of the kitchen sink—her island in a sea of tile, even if it was a bit too small for her ninety-pound bulk. I wrapped my arms around him from behind and nuzzled his shoulder.

"I'm heading to bed," I said.

He swiveled carefully and wrapped me in a tight embrace. "Goodnight, sweetie."

As he began to release me and turn away, I leaned in and pulled him closer, pressing against him. He tossed away the dish cloth he was holding and responded eagerly, one hand running along my jawline and lifting my chin to cover my mouth with a kiss, the other hand running through my hair and down my back. We stumbled down the hall to our bedroom and closed the door on Holly, close behind as always, and her steps tapped back to her bed in the living room.

"Aww, poor Holly," Michael mumbled between kisses down my side. I giggled and told him to shut up, and we tumbled into bed together.

Afterwards, when I began to drift to sleep, he stirred. "Honey," he whispered. "I'm not tired yet. I'm going to stay up a little while longer."

"Okay," I mumbled into my pillow. "Just don't wake me up, please."

"I'll try. Love you."

"Love you, too."

He kissed my head, got out of bed, and crept out of the room. Sleep came quickly.

I didn't hear him come back. But later that night, I woke to his weight in bed behind me and his arm wrapped around me. We weren't normally ones to sleep in each other's arms and I didn't want to be woken up, but I was too sleepy to care. I accepted the embrace and began falling back to sleep.

Then his hand began to move up and down my side; a familiar, reassuring touch when we sat together watching a movie or talking, but in that moment a disruptive movement, dragging me further from sleep. I had already stayed up later than usual and expected a wine headache in the morning. I pleaded inwardly for him to stop.

I moved my hand to lay on top of his, deliberately stopping his motion, willing him to be still, and began to drift away again. His hand moved under my shirt and snaked across my bare stomach, his arm tightening possessively around my waist, his groin pressing against my backside.

I'd never been someone who could wake up in a good mood, and Michael knew it. Pulled so forcefully from sleep yet again, I pushed him away, flinging his arm from around me and scooting toward my edge of the bed to widen the space between us. He didn't protest or move to close the gap. To my relief, I was left in peace the rest of the night.

I didn't mention it to him the next day. Maybe I felt guilty about the rejection, or maybe I didn't want to make him feel bad for being affectionate. But I thought I should let it go.

Chapter Three

A FEW DAYS LATER, I got home to find Michael busy in the workshop behind the house building a wooden bench for the front porch.

"But we never sit on the front porch," I had said when he told me his plans.

"That's because we don't have a bench there," he'd answered with a grin.

"Hi, wife!" he called when I appeared at the door.

Holly trotted over to me and pressed her nose into the side of my leg as her dutiful greeting, then returned to her place on the floor in Michael's shadow. I glanced at her muddy nose and was grateful I'd worn black slacks.

I approached Michael and bent to kiss him, but before I had a chance to say anything, he spoke.

"Now, don't be mad . . . " he paused dramatically.

I straightened, and my heart pounded while I waited.

My hand drifted to the hair at the base of my neck and I twisted it, pulling until it hurt. I tried to make it look like I was rubbing a sore spot on my neck or playing casually with my hair while I tugged hard enough to make the pain a distraction.

Michael continued to stare at his work, as if he had forgotten whatever he was going to say. His brow furrowed and he leaned closer to the work table, squinting at the wood. He ran a finger over a blemish, sanded it, then rubbed it again.

I couldn't keep the possibilities from storming through my mind. Maybe he'd said something he knew would embarrass me to one of my coworkers, or shared something overly personal. My stomach roiled at the thought, and I dug my nails into the skin where my scalp met my neck. Increasing the pain, increasing the distraction.

Maybe it was me who had acted badly. Maybe the wine had got to me more than I'd realized, and I said or did something inappropriate without knowing it.

Or if it wasn't the happy hour, what else could it be? Did he hear me talking to Ivy? As the seconds crept by, my mind began to stretch back as far as our wedding night a few weeks earlier and how drunk we were at the reception. I'd been meeting many of Michael's extended family members and old friends for the first time. God, what if he'd lied to spare my feelings when I asked if they could tell I'd had too much to drink?

I tried to wait for him to end his tortuously long pause, but after a few more moments, I broke.

"What did you have to tell me?" I asked. I forced my voice to sound casual.

"I bought honey wheat instead of whole wheat today." He finally looked up from his work and grinned at me.

As I expected. Michael being Michael. I willed my heart to slow. "Great," I said, rolling my eyes. "You do know I'm a nut job and that when you say things like that I assume you have our neighbor's body in the garage or something, right?"

"Ha! Yeah, I like to make you sweat."

I approached his stool and he rose to kiss me. I wondered if he meant it a little, if he knew how much that kind of teasing got to me. An actual bead of sweat was trickling down the center of my back and the tingling relief that cooled my body as soon as he finished his joke made me notice the damp under my arms, and I wondered what he would think of me if he knew it was really that easy, that I wasn't as good at taking it as I pretended to be.

But like so many things about me, I didn't want him to know.

"What do you think?" He gestured to his project, still in the early stages, printed images and diagrams scattered about with his notes scrawled in the margins. But he wanted my opinion on the wood, not the plans. I reached out and ran my fingers across the freshly cut pieces, loving the smooth feel and the clean smell of it.

"I think it's going to be beautiful," I said truthfully.

"Red cedar, like you suggested," he said.

"I see that. It's perfect. You are planning to use a transparent stain, right?" The wood had faint streaks and swirls of red and pink that were so lovely I already felt protective of them.

"I figured I'd leave that step to you," he said.

"Perfect." I had hoped he would say that.

He glanced around the workshop. "You're not in the middle of anything right now, are you?"

"No. Ivy is on the lookout for some kind of coffee table with storage that she can put on her patio. I'm hoping she finds a nice beaten up one for me, with weird drawers and nooks and crannies. But until she finds something, I'm all yours."

Michael had picked up building furniture from his father, and when we started dating I had taken an interest. But while I remained intimidated by building pieces from scratch, I always enjoyed helping with the finishing touches. It had turned into a hobby of my own and I liked restoring old and abused items, giving them life again.

"You're such a weirdo." He shook his head at me in mock sadness. "I'm offering you a brand-new, sturdy piece of furniture to work on, and you shrug and play it cool, like you could take the job or leave it. While you and I both know how excited you're going to be when your sister comes along to hand you a pile of moldy sticks."

I laughed. "Your bench is going to be wonderful before I even touch it. I like watching the transformation."

His mouth dropped open. "And here I was thinking it was *our* bench." He sniffed loudly, his voice breaking theatrically.

"Oh god, I'm so sorry." I threw my hand over my heart and placed the other solemnly on the wood. "Future bench, I promise to love you more than my sister's coffee table."

"There, was that so hard?" He flopped back down onto his stool, shoulders slumped, and shook his head at me again. "I can't deny having my doubts about how much you meant that. But it's a start, at least."

It was like that with Michael. Just when I started to think his melodrama was annoying, he would make me remember that I loved even that about him. It had been like that from the beginning—me stressing out about insignificant things like where a piece of furniture would go, him teasing me and making my worries seem silly.

***

"It's not weird is it, us having a church wedding?"

I asked Michael that same question probably ten times in the course of planning our wedding. The last time was maybe a week before the date, too late to change anything anyway. We were sprawled out on the bed on a lazy Saturday afternoon, a forgotten television show paused so long the screen had gone blue, Michael on his stomach while I lay on my back at his side, one of my legs threaded through his.

"Would you rather do it somewhere else?" he asked.

"No, it's not that. A church is traditional. It would be nice. It's just...people won't think it's weird, since neither of us go anymore?"

"Oh, I dunno. It hasn't been that long for me. Only since I moved out of my parents' house, then a couple times my first year of college. So only...Jesus, I guess that is like eight years. Holy shit, we're like, adult adults."

We grinned at each other.

"Way longer for me," I said. "I think I was five or six the last time, maybe?"

Church had been one of the first things to go when my mother's anxiety began to worsen. And when she died many years later, Ivy planned everything and we had her service outside at the cemetery. So the memories I had of church were dim; the sprawling sanctuary lined with polished pews, the fresh scent of carpet cleaner mixed with that new-book smell from the hymnals placed neatly in every seat, the floor to ceiling windows. I know now it was a relatively simple church, but at the time I thought it was a mansion. I imagined wealthy people had homes like that; huge living rooms lined with more couches than they could ever use. And when we stopped going, it felt like being cut off from a world where everyone acted happy and kind and everything was clean and well-kept.

"Well, I don't think our attendance record is going to be part of the ceremony," he said. "I was planning on working it into my vows of course, something about loving you in spite of your lapses, maybe something about being sad you might go to hell but finding acceptance—*ow*!"

I poked him in the ribs, grinning as he rubbed his side. "What?" He continued, "I think it'll segue nicely from the monologue I prepared about how living in sin was your idea."

"You know what I mean," I said, poking him again.

"I know, I know. But who cares? It's about what we want, not what anyone else thinks. You're sure it is what you want? It's not because my parents care about church, is it? Because they'd never say anything either way. And I don't care where we do it. A park, the backyard, your office has a nice view over that parking lot . . . "

"It is a breathtaking parking lot," I agreed.

He pulled himself up to his elbows and planted a kiss on my cheek, and I knew he was happy I was smiling instead of being stressed out, that he was allowed to joke and keep us both from taking the wedding too seriously, and we both glowed with satisfaction over how well we were working together.

"I do want a church wedding," I said. "It's traditional." *It's normal.* "And churches are pretty."

"Great. Then that's what we'll do." He rolled over onto his side and ran his hand through my hair. "Are you excited to look at the house tomorrow?"

We were still living in my apartment then. Michael had moved in with me when his lease ran out, and we'd started looking for a house when we got engaged a few months later.

"I am," I said. "I hope this one is more like the pictures."

"Me, too. You don't think it's too far out? You're the one with a commute."

"Forty-five minutes isn't that bad," I said.

I knew how much it meant to him to have a little space. Michael had grown up on a hobby farm near St. Louis, and he once told me proudly that he had seen four different kinds of animals give birth. I wasn't sure if he was trying to amuse me or impress me. But with Michael, it was usually both.

Chapter Four

WHEN IT HAPPENED again, I woke to a sharp squeeze and his arm clamped across my stomach. His hand began to move, swift and insistent, up my side and down over my hip and thigh and back up my side, caressing and rubbing me. I couldn't understand what he was thinking. I had been dead asleep.

His hand moved up my back and then my neck. He raked his fingers through my hair and I opened my eyes completely as he began twisting the strands around his fingers, the pressure not so hard as to be painful but enough to tug my head a little backward.

I had no patience for being woken up so abruptly again. I elbowed him in the ribs and pushed him away. As before, he stayed where he was and didn't touch me again. I felt him shift in the bed behind me, then lie there silently. I kept my back to him and fell back to sleep.

When I woke up, I was surprised to find that I had moved into his space during the night and was curled in a cozy ball against his back. Falling asleep annoyed with him, I expected to wake feeling the same, but my subconscious betrayed me. I was irritated before I opened my eyes, unsure how to broach the topic with him or what to say. Twice in a single week he'd tried to wake me up for sex long after I had gone to sleep—and on work nights.

I wondered if that was normal for other couples. I had a boyfriend once who worked at a bar and came over to wake me up at crazy hours. But I'd been in college, no long commute and early morning meetings, and we'd always agreed on those plans ahead of time.

I kissed Michael awake before I left and, looking at his peaceful, rested face, clear of any guilt or worry, I wondered if he realized what he was doing. Maybe he was doing it in his sleep.

"How'd you sleep?" He stretched and sat up in bed beside me.

He was shirtless, as he usually slept, the blankets in a messy bunch around him, his wavy hair tangled in one spot on the side of his head.

"Not well," I said, almost apologetic. "You woke me up again."

"Did I really?" His eyebrows furrowed and he looked unhappy. "I thought I was quiet coming in. I'm sorry."

"It wasn't when you came in that was the problem," I said. "It was the cuddling."

"Cuddling?"

"Yes. You were moving so much when you came to bed, and you did it a few nights ago, too. I don't know if you've done it before and I usually sleep through it or what, but when you rub my side and move so much and squeeze me, it wakes me up. And it's one thing to be spontaneous, but I'm generally not in the mood when I'm passed out, you know?"

I'm not sure what I expected. Embarrassment, confusion, irritation? I did not expect him to laugh out loud in my face. It startled me and I leaned away from him, indignant.

Did he think it was funny?

"I did not squeeze or rub you at all," he said. "I know that would wake you up. Sometimes when I come to bed and you're sleeping, I give you a light kiss on the forehead or cheek before rolling over to my side and passing out, but that's it. I did that last night, just a peck on your head."

He had the nerve to tap the top of my head with his index finger as he spoke, and I flinched at the condescending touch.

He grinned into my glare, unconcerned. Playful, benign. "Then I went to my side and slept with my back to you all night," he said. "I didn't hug you or anything. Who are you dreaming about?" His tone became mischievous and suggestive.

Is he implying these are sex dreams? Seriously? I'm upset about losing sleep, and he's making it a joke.

"Well, it was *about* you." My tone gained a slight edge. "If it was a dream at all. Maybe you're doing it in your sleep."

He laughed again, and a rush of embarrassment flamed from my stomach to my face. "No," he said with amused certainty. "I think I'd have heard about it a lot earlier if I was in the habit of feeling women up in my sleep. Besides, I was up pretty late last night. I passed right out when I came up."

"How late?" I asked.

"I'm not sure. It might've been after two."

His vagueness made me think it was probably closer to three. *So much for keeping regular hours.*

He didn't seem to notice I was still bothered, and even if he had asked, I probably couldn't have clearly communicated why. If they were only dreams, they lingered and left little traces of irritation like dreams of arguments do, even though the dreamer knows the arguments were only in their mind. I was annoyed he was so sure it wasn't him, annoyed he didn't seem to think it mattered either way, annoyed about him staying up too late, annoyed I was having these weird dreams in the first place, and annoyed that I was letting them get under my skin.

In other words, I've woken up on the wrong side of the bed and should probably shut up.

And so I tucked my feelings away as we said our goodbyes for the day. But the image of Michael that was not actually Michael, standing in the doorway watching me, walking toward me as I slept, had not faded from my mind. Nor had the pressure of his arm wrapped so firmly around my ribs that I almost couldn't breathe, his fingers kneading my hip bone, his nose nestling into my hair, and his breath on my neck.

***

I sent Michael a brief message that afternoon to let him know I wouldn't be coming home right after work. Our house was outside of St. Louis, in a neighborhood that had probably been called living "in the country" a few years earlier, though it was rapidly evolving into another suburb of the city. Ivy lived and worked inside the city near my job, so I saw her often for lunch, on the way home from work, or when I ran to the city on errands.

I stopped by her bookshop after work. I barely glanced at the main room, already so familiar to me with its floor-to-ceiling shelves and a couple customers dragging their fingers over books on opposite sides, and I turned straight into the small side room. Ivy looked up from her perch in the window seat. She nodded at the drink cart in the corner that I had already begun to move toward. Once we were settled together in the nook, me sipping coffee and Ivy herbal tea, I began updating her about my work—I had a secret, one-sided rivalry with another manager named Julieta, who had the habit of talking over me in meetings and seemed to usually say everything I had wanted to say, only better.

I was convinced that Devin was in love with her, but I could only be petty enough to gossip about it with Ivy. When I'd finished listing that week's lingering looks and Devin's awkward throat clearing in Julieta's presence, Ivy began updating me about the bookshop.

"Some freshly graduated asshat dropped in the other day to introduce himself as a fellow indie bookshop owner," she said. "I guess he's opening his place right around the corner and wanted to talk to me about keeping our competition friendly and collaborative." She used exaggerated gestures to form air quotes and rolled her eyes as she spoke. "He started going on and on about how he wants his bookshop to be an experience, not 'just' a bookshop—I guess mine is 'just' a bookshop—and he started assuring me that he's going to have a huge selection of books written by 'diverse' authors. Like mine's Dead White Guy central? Please. I don't know if he wanted me to thank him or what."

"What did you say to that?" I found myself leaning forward eagerly.

"I said 'How nice for you!' and I don't think he understood the sarcasm because he smiled like a fool when I said it. But I was too irritated to think of anything better."

"He sounds insufferable. Are you worried?"

"No, I don't think so. I'd be all for the area turning into a book town. And I'd have appreciated him reaching out if he wasn't such a pretentious little shit about it. Oh, be right back!" She ran off to help a customer who had casually leaned across the doorway to see if anyone was around to check them out.

"I've been having weird dreams about Michael," I said when Ivy came back.

"Weird like how?" The suggestive tilt in her voice was clear and I had to ignore the flash of irritation that ran through me. Why did everyone assume I was having sex dreams? And why would I be running around telling everyone about them if I were?

"Not good weird." I cleared my throat. "The first one was a couple of weeks ago, I think. It didn't seem like a big deal at the time. I dreamed that I woke up and he was standing in the bedroom doorway. It was four a.m., which stuck out to me since it was so late, but I went back to sleep as he was walking toward the bed. The next day, I asked him why he came to bed so late, and he said he was in bed by midnight."

I couldn't help but feel a slight thrill of satisfaction when her eyes lost their playful glint and brightened with interest instead.

"Oh, that's a little creepy," she said.

"It was! It stuck in my mind more than I expected, the way he just . . . stood there for a minute, like he was watching me. And then I had a couple more dreams where I thought Michael came to bed and he was hugging me while I slept and rubbing me. Trying to initiate something, I guess. But then he told me it wasn't him."

"Seriously? He says he doesn't hug you at night at all?"

"Pretty much. We don't usually cuddle at night. And he was squeezing me and massaging my back even though I was dead asleep and had to work the next day."

Ivy laughed. "So, what? You're saying he wants sex when he comes to bed?"

A pang of embarrassment hit me at her dismissiveness, and my head darted toward the door to the main room to see if any customers were around. "Even if it was that, I wouldn't appreciate him trying it when I'm asleep in the middle of the night. He knows I get cranky about being woken up. But he says he didn't do it. That's what's weird about it. It didn't feel like a dream, so I don't know. I don't know what's going on in my head."

"Do you think he's doing it in his sleep without realizing it?"

"Maybe," I said. "But it doesn't make sense that he would start doing that now, when he never has before. Plus, that wouldn't explain the first dream. Standing in the doorway. He's not a sleepwalker."

"So you're just having weird dreams then."

I shrugged. "I guess. I'm sure I'm the crazy one in this, like always."

She smiled, but her next words came like a soft admonishment. "A few nightmares meaning you're crazy is a stretch. Besides, marriage is a big change. I'm sure all kinds of weird shit comes out in a couple's first years." She allowed a beat to pass before adding with a bigger smile, "Or your house is haunted."

It wasn't meant as a serious suggestion, I didn't think—sometimes it was hard to tell with Ivy. But I humored the idea, as though it was necessary to rule it out. I tucked my feet under myself, mirroring her position, and stared out the window for a moment.

"We lived there together for a year before we got married, and the dreams just started," I said.

"Good point. Well, next time it happens, try to make yourself wake up completely and confront him. In case it isn't a dream and it is him. Show him what he's doing." Then, as an afterthought, "And even if you are dreaming, the best thing would still be to make yourself wake up, right?"

"Sure. I'll try. That whole pinching thing has never worked for me, though."

"Ugh, me either. Every nightmare I've had, I just have to wait for it to play out."

***

That night was different. There was no hugging, no rubbing—only a conversation.

My sleep was shallow. I opened my eyes the moment the doorknob clicked with a light rattle. He came into the room silently, creeping toward the bed, trying to avoid making noise.

I shifted slightly and turned toward him so he could see I was awake. I couldn't see his face in the dark, but he straightened from his hunched, cautious position when he realized I wasn't sleeping, and approached my side of the bed instead of his. He sat beside me and laid his hand on my arm, leaning in and kissing me on the forehead.

"Hi," he whispered.

"Hi." His presence was comforting, bringing with it a slight relief that he was coming to bed before I had a chance to dream. I glanced at the clock and saw it wasn't yet midnight. I wondered if he was trying to make a habit of coming to bed earlier, and the thought pleased me.

I wondered if he was worried about me.

"Can't sleep?" he asked. His voice was low and scratchy, barely above a whisper, as though he couldn't adjust to the idea of making too much noise while I was in bed, regardless of whether I was awake or not.

"I think I had just fallen asleep."

"Did I wake you?"

"It's okay," I said, and meant it. "I wasn't sleeping deeply yet."

But even as I said it, I was being carried back to darkness, my eyes closing heavily.

"Sleep well," I thought I heard him say, his voice disappearing in a low murmur. I was aware only of his hand continuing to gently stroke my arm, then my hair, as I drifted to sleep.

The next day, I wondered if it was a dream.

Chapter Five

THE DAY OF Michael's birthday, I woke with my breath lodged in my throat, frozen halfway through a noisy yawn and a careless stretch that threatened to brush against him. Consciousness hit me like a wave and I exhaled, gingerly folding my limbs back into my body and withdrawing from his space. I glided noiselessly from the bed and felt the floor for my sweatpants, palms pressing blindly against the carpet until I found them. I held my breath as I left the room, eyes glued to his still form, watching and listening for any sign that he was waking.

Once safely in the hall, I pranced through the house, gleeful at my successful escape and almost giddy in my excitement to surprise him. Holly dragged herself from her bed in the living room and I let her outside on my way to the kitchen.

Michael's first birthday after we got married fell on a Wednesday, the bland middle of our work week. The real celebrating would come later, with every friend he could scrape together crammed into our house that Saturday, which I believed I did a great job at pretending not to dread. The least I could do for his thirtieth. On Wednesday, though, I knew he would expect nothing. I hadn't even had to lie to him about not being able to take it off because he never asked me to. He assumed I would work and that we would do some small celebration that evening. He'd probably have been happy to get a good meal out of the affair, and in his mind, a good meal could be as simple as a well-made burger and some fries.

But I wanted that birthday to be memorable. The first special occasion of our marriage. I took the day off without telling him, and planned on surprising him with an indulgent breakfast of crepes filled with cheesy eggs, plus hash browns and fresh fruit. Once the food settled, I planned for us to go hiking through the wooded trails nearby that we had been talking about wanting to explore since we moved in but hadn't made the time.

I let Holly back in, and she laid down in the living room, watching me with little interest. Holly and I were on friendly terms, but she was not mine and I was not hers. She seemed to enjoy my company when Michael wasn't around, but I was next to invisible to her when we were all in the same room. Her worshipful eyes followed him and him alone, and her place was at his side whenever that was an option.

I lined the counter with my supplies and hoped he wouldn't wake up before I finished and catch me in the act. The kitchen was far enough from the bedroom that I could make noise without worrying. The front door of our house opened into an entryway that led straight into a large square living room, with a hallway to the right that connected to a spare bedroom and a bathroom, ending with our master. Turning left led to the kitchen and dining area. In the living room, there was a staircase to the second floor, which included Michael's office and another spare room we used for working out.

I loved our house. That morning, I felt the kind of contentment that can only come with a slight edge of nerves because it's all too good. I stared out the kitchen windows as I prepared the coffee. The morning was shaping up to be beautiful, with pink light filtering through the green, orange-tinged grove. On days like that, I would look around and still not believe it was mine. Michael had never seen the place where I grew up. The small trailer house, the muddy patch of chain-linked earth that held it, the dirty windows that stared uninvitingly at the cracked pavement of a street crammed too closely with other small houses, muddy patches, and dirty windows.

He knew about it, but it was different to see it.

He'd never met any of my family, aside from Ivy. My mother died shortly after we started dating—late enough in our relationship for him to offer to go with me to her funeral, and still early enough for me to have the relief of saying no. I was glad he never had the chance to meet her, glad to keep him from the rest of my family. Not because I was ashamed, though maybe I was a little ashamed; but mostly because I wanted to let go, to enjoy the life that was turning out so much better than I had dared to hope.

I tried so very hard not to fear my happiness.

Breakfast took longer than I expected, so I was a little surprised to find him still sleeping soundly by the time I'd finished and sneaked into the bedroom to wake him. I set a mug of coffee softly on his nightstand and got under the covers. A pleasant tingle ran through me at the temperature change as I moved into the pocket of warmth his sleeping body had created. He stirred and wrapped his arms around me, and I wished I could stay there, almost regretting that there was a hot breakfast waiting for us.

"Happy birthday," I said, my voice soft, pulling him gently into the day.

"Thank you," he said through a yawn. "Are you going in late?"

"I took the day off. Surprise."

"Did you really?" His voice brightened and sounded more awake.

"I did. And I made a huge breakfast, so we should go eat it."

"Oh?" he asked, interested. "What'd you make?"

"Everything."

"Sounds perfect."

I nodded. "And this afternoon, I thought we could go hiking with Holly. We can finally check out those trails we've been talking about since we moved in. You know, one of the selling points of getting this house. 'Get out into nature,' we said. 'We'll take hikes every day that it's nice,' we said."

He laughed softly, and I continued. "And then we can do anything else you want to do. It's your day." I pulled myself up onto my elbow and kissed his nose. "Sound good?"

"Perfect," he said again.

But instead of getting up, he held me close and nuzzled my neck. "Or we could stay right here." He pulled the covers over our heads and engulfed me in a cocoon of his heat, one hand traveling up my back and the other grabbing my hip and pressing me into him.

I wanted nothing more than to stay in bed and give in to his exploring hands and soft, dry kisses along my neck, making love all morning, and I was filled with sudden dismay that I hadn't planned for it. How hadn't I foreseen that? Of course he would want to spend a rare morning together with no responsibilities like this.

But the stove was on.

Feeling like an idiot, I pulled away gently. "The food," I apologized.

"It'll still be good in a little while," he said.

"It won't. There are eggs, they'll get hard, and the stove is on . . . "

He let me pull away with regret in his eyes, and I felt like I was ruining his birthday before it had started, the old fear creeping in that everything I did was wrong. "I'm sorry," I said. "I didn't think . . . "

"Sweetie, don't apologize for making me breakfast." He kissed me and hopped out of bed.

We made our way to the kitchen and after Holly gave him a much more enthusiastic greeting than she had spared for me, tail wagging frantically and nose sniffing him from waist to toes as if to make sure nothing had changed in the night, Michael looked around at the spread I had prepared.

He grinned. "You went all out. Thank you, sweetie."

"Happy birthday." I kissed him and began preparing our plates.

It took over an hour after eating before either of us was up for moving again, time we spent relaxing on our screened-in back porch while I tried to stop myself from asking him again and again if he was sure there wasn't something else he'd rather do, or from being anxious about the fact that I seemed to have overfed us into a torpor, or from worrying that his special birthday might turn out to be very boring after all. He stepped away for a few minutes at a time to accept calls from his brother Elliot, then his mom, then his dad. When he finished the last call with thank you's and I love you's, he set his phone on the rail with determination.

"All right," he said, "anyone else who wants to tell me happy birthday can do it in a text message like a normal human being." He dropped down next to me. "I'm all yours for the rest of the day."

"It's your birthday," I told him. "Other way around."

We rocked slowly on the wooden swing, the morning starting to feel like so many other weekend mornings spent in similar fashion. Growing up, Michael's family had a tradition they called "coffee time". Coffee time happened every morning, and it consisted of the family having coffee together and talking.

"Is that it?" I had asked when Michael first explained it to me.

"That's it," he had said.

"You just talk, like you do every day, and about nothing in particular, but you call it coffee time . . . because you're holding coffee while you do it?" I didn't mean to tease him, but his family always sounded ridiculously perfect.

"Well, we do drink the coffee," he answered dryly. "It's not *about* the coffee, it's about making time in your day without distractions to talk to your family."

"The coffee isn't a distraction?"

"Coffee is never a distraction," he answered gravely.

It sounded so simple and almost comically wholesome to me, and it delighted me to continue the tradition with him when we could. But that morning, I was sure it was boring and all I could think about was how his birthday wasn't turning out as special as I had hoped.

My spirits lifted the moment we started our hike. It was a crisp, sunny fall day and the trail was flanked on both sides by orange and red trees. The trail traced a river that came in and out of view through the trees to our right, at times close enough to step away and dip our hands in it if we wanted, at other times separated by wild, impassable undergrowth and trees. Most of the first half was uphill, and by an hour into the climb, the views to our left were beginning to look down into valleys and hills filled with trees, broken by rocky dips and small cliffs.

At one point, the land on our left dropped suddenly and we paused, looking out over the edge to take in the view together. The tightly packed, colorful trees stretched beyond our sight. It was hard to believe such boundless wilderness existed in the same world as humans at all, much less such a short distance from a sprawling city. Suddenly Michael grabbed me by the wrist and spun me into his chest and kissed me.

"I didn't think I wanted to do anything today, but this is awesome. Thank you." His dark eyes, frank and unabashed, stared into mine and I loved that he never thought anything of telling me exactly what he was thinking. I thought that the cliche I'd heard old married couples say was true, that I did love him so much more after the years we had known each other than when we were first falling in love, and in that moment, I trusted that I would continue to love him more each year.

"I haven't even given you your actual present yet," I said. "And we shouldn't wait for birthdays to do things like this. This is beautiful."

"Agreed." He stepped away toward the river. "I have to piss," he said unceremoniously.

I rolled my eyes with a slight smile and turned back toward the view while Michael disappeared into the woods behind me, Holly close behind him. The trees were spread out on that side, so they continued for a while before disappearing, and silence fell around me.

We hadn't seen a single other person on the trail, which wasn't too surprising on a weekday, but now I noticed a figure moving through a small side trail in the woods far below me. There was something familiar about him, and I stared openly. It seemed unlikely that he would look up in my direction and even if he did, I wasn't sure that he could see me from his lowered vantage point anyway. But he did look up, and he looked right at me. I froze. It was Michael.

I reeled and took a step back from the ledge, my vision spinning, confronted with an absolute impossibility. I put a hand on a tree to steady myself and looked back out. He was still staring up at me, blatant and unmoving. After another moment that seemed to drag on without end, the figure looked back down and continued moving along his trail. It ran parallel to mine for a time, though I could see it would soon twist away deeper into the trees and disappear in the shadows.

No. Not Michael, I thought. It couldn't be. Just a distant figure in the trees.

Michael hadn't been gone from my side for long. Even if he had sprinted through the brush down the trail far enough so I wouldn't see him cross it to the other side and then scampered down the steep hill . . . Then there was Holly . . . No. There was no way it could've been Michael.

The man was far away and I couldn't see him clearly. I was thinking of Michael, so I saw Michael.

I spun as I heard him approaching from behind and was relieved when he appeared, Holly in tow.

"Hi," he said simply.

"Hi. I finally saw someone else out here," I said, hoping I didn't sound accusatory.

"You did? Where?"

"Down in the woods," I said, pointing. He was gone. Somehow, I knew he would be gone. "On that little dirt trail. Seems like a creepy place to hike. But the weird thing was, he kind of looked like you."

"Looked like me how?"

I struggled to answer. 'He had your face' would sound a bit dramatic.

"I don't know," I said. "He was far away and in the shadows. I guess he was a similar height and body type or something."

"So you were looking at his body?" He grinned at me impishly.

"I only thought he was you for a second." I shook my head but smiled at him and continued down the trail.

I couldn't stop tracing the distance in my mind—down the trail, around the corner, down the hill, then back again. Michael was in good shape, but there was no way.

Not possible. Why am I even analyzing it so thoroughly?

It was starting to feel like my own husband haunted me, a figure in the darkness and shadows, dogging my every step, sleeping and waking, night and day.

CHAPTER SIX

MY SLEEP CONTINUED to be disturbed. Some nights were uneventful, but others were plagued by dreams within dreams—squeezed, rubbed, pawed at, and shaken, then waking up and telling Michael to leave me alone only to be told the next day that I hadn't woken up at all, we hadn't spoken; confusing layers of reality I could only attempt to sort out in the light of day.

"What time did you come to bed last night?"

It became an almost daily question. I tried to ask it casually, and Michael always seemed to answer it without hesitation, unaware of the extra questions hidden in the folds.

Are you messing with me?

Are you lying to me?

Am I losing it?

But he was blind to the tension, or pretended to be.

Then one night his hand ran up my back and through my hair again, rubbing my scalp in a pleasant circular motion for a moment. A sleepy, happy moan escaped my lips. It was so relaxing I didn't mind the late hour.

His hand slowly began to tighten into a fistful of my hair. And he began to pull.

This again? I started to scoot away from him when he jerked his hand with unexpected force, yanking my head back and sending pain shooting through my scalp. I reacted blindly, furious. My arm flew back in the darkness and my elbow connected with his face. His muffled yelp of pain and surprise filled me with guilt, which I swallowed, burying the automatic urge to apologize and see if he was okay.

He deserved it. He hurt me.

I couldn't believe Michael had hurt me. I was vibrating with the rush of adrenaline, yet I laid still, scared to move, waiting to see what would happen.

He rose and stalked out of the room without a word. I stayed where I was, tormented, torn between letting him stew alone and following him, and not knowing if I would be following to check on him or to yell at him. My mind was a blur and my eyes stung with tears.

What does this mean for us?

I don't remember wiping away my tears or making a decision about what to do. I don't remember deciding to stay where I was and go back to sleep, but somehow, that's what happened. The next thing I remembered was waking up with a start to a sunlit room. An empty room.

Michael's side of the bed lay bare and undisturbed.

I wasn't sure which of us was supposed to be mad, but decided in an instant that if he was angry, I would be angrier.

I pulled on a robe and checked the mirror, smoothing my hair and making sure my face was clear. The last thing I needed was to walk into an argument looking as unhinged as I felt. I headed down the hallway, and with some apprehension began climbing the stairs after glances into the spare bedroom and at the living room couch told me he wasn't there.

I was about halfway up the stairs when I heard his voice and froze. It drifted from his office in soft snatches. "I don't know, it's not like I expected."

A pause.

"No, not in a bad way. Just different from what I expected."

I realized he was probably talking to his brother like he did almost every day, and started to continue up the stairs, but something held me.

What was different? Our marriage? Was he talking about me? Was I not measuring up?

I took one more silent step, straining to hear, but I could tell after a moment that the conversation had moved on and they were saying goodbye. When he finished his call, I took a deep breath and closed the remaining distance to his office with quick, sure steps and pushed open the door that was hanging ajar.

He was sitting at his computer, Holly curled up in her usual place under his desk. I took in his crumpled clothes, the clothes he wore yesterday—*would he have come to bed at all in those clothes?*—and the cold coffee in his hand and his unshaven face. He looked exactly as I had found him on so many other mornings when he had gotten too engrossed in work or a side project to pull himself away. He looked up and gave me a guilty smile, but a smile nonetheless, a familiar smile that said, 'You caught me. I've messed up my schedule again.' I glanced over his face and noted the lack of bruises or marks. It was not a face that had been elbowed.

Another dream.

So this weirdness is me. All me.

"You stayed up all night?" I asked.

"Yeah, sorry," he said, rising to hug me and kiss my cheek. "I went down a rabbit hole with the new website; they're trying to get it live before next semester. How did you sleep?"

"Another visit from Creepy Michael," I said with a rueful smile, trying to make light of it.

And now I've gone and named it.

"I'm sorry," he said, then added ominously, "Maybe someone's breaking in."

"Sure, and he's wearing your face?" I regretted the words immediately, my stomach doing a light flip as I realized that I never saw his face clearly in the darkness.

But I always knew it was Michael. His hands, his breath, his body against mine, the feel of his lips when they brushed my neck. After years of only Michael, the touch of anyone else would be startling, different, alien. No one but Michael was featured in these dreams.

"I *have* checked the house since you started having these dreams, and everything's safe," he said. "Unless he's living in our bedroom walls, pretty sure he's not real."

"Great," I said. "Now I'll probably dream about a figure living in our walls and coming from hidden panels next to our bed after we fall asleep."

"I'm sorry," he said again. "We don't have paneling, if that helps. What was the dream about last night?"

"You pulled my hair, and I elbowed you in the face." My eyes involuntarily traveled over his clear face again.

"Oh, no. I would never pull your hair," he said, wrapping his arms around me, running his hand gently along my jawline and kissing my temple, then gathering the strands of my hair that fell at the side of my face and kissing them, then the top of my head. "Unless you wanted me to." His tone became suggestive.

I smiled up at him and said, "I have to get ready for work. And I don't think you should look to Creepy Michael for pointers."

He kissed me again and sat back down. "Well, the good news is, I'll definitely come to bed early tonight. I'm going to stay up all day today to get my schedule back on track."

"Good," I said. "Maybe some of these dreams are because I don't sleep as well without you."

"Aww. I'll try to be better about coming to bed."

I started to leave to get ready for work when Michael's head popped back up as though he remembered something. "Hey, I talked to my mom last night and they're thinking of visiting soon," he said. "Maybe the weekend after next."

"Oh, that sounds good." The prospect of having house guests was always a little stressful, but his parents were nice people who had welcomed me into their family with an openness beyond anything I ever expected. They were spending most of their retirement in Florida, which was where Elliot was going to graduate school. We managed to see them several times a year, mostly because they made frequent trips to St. Louis.

"They might stay for three or four days," he said, "But I told them you'll only be off the weekend since we used a bunch of time off for the honeymoon."

"Yeah, I should probably save my time for the holidays," I agreed, trying not to be jealous of Michael's flexibility. I had benefits I knew were above average, but since Michael had complete control of his schedule and workload, his free time was virtually unlimited. It was a little weird to me that his job had barely changed in years, and he seemed to care more about his side projects volunteering his time to help nonprofits improve their websites and programs. He could have easily qualified for a leadership role with an actual company but had no interest.

Sometimes it worried me that he wasn't more ambitious. That since he had always had enough, he didn't seem to have the same need I've always had to improve, to make his life better. But sometimes, when taking time off made me worry my office would grind to a halt or when I realized my entire workday had been filled with performance reviews and emails instead of the work I enjoyed, I wondered if he wasn't onto something.

***

That day, I had a meeting first thing in the morning with a high-profile client who had the ability to make me feel like a child playing pretend at my job. I had long ago cleansed my speech of the thick twang that was common in my impoverished Alabama hometown, yet the first time I spoke to him, I was sure he could hear trailer park in my voice. I had been dressing professionally ever since I graduated from college, yet the first time he looked at me, I was certain he knew I grew up in hand-me-downs and dollar store tank tops.

I took extra care getting ready that day and chose one of my pricier outfits, though I couldn't have said what made it expensive beyond the store where I bought it. It was a simple sheath dress that I hoped was professional and flattering, paired with a cream-colored blazer. I tried not to worry that the outfit would go from feeling stylish to coarse and ill-fitting once his eyes were on it.

My client's name was Charles Jacob Worthing V and, like his name, he reeked of old money. It almost made it worse that he wasn't pompous, entitled, irresponsible, or in any other way undeserving of the money that had been in his family for generations—wealth he had increased exponentially over his long lifetime. Instead he was friendly, intelligent, and exceedingly charitable. He relied on our firm for most of his companies' financial consulting needs, from taxes and audits to any other issues they came across. Most people only think of the taxes portion when they hear 'accounting', but my team's focus was on fraud prevention.

I sometimes imagined Mr. Worthing saying, his pale blue eyes narrowing as he peered into mine, *So you're supposed to make sure no one's stealing from me, but who's making sure* you're *not stealing from me?*

In spite of the swirling insecurities and mad scenarios churning in my mind, my spine was straight and my chin was level as I was shown into his office. I met his eyes without faltering.

"Mr. Worthing, it's good to see you," I said, convincing enough that I almost believed myself. "Thanks for making time today."

Do you even know why that dress you bought was so expensive? Or can you not even tell the difference between it and the rest of your clothes? The Mr. Worthing in my head shook his head at me, sad and knowing.

"Ms. Brookes, thank you for making the trip down here." Mr. Worthing in reality was smiling kindly and stood to shake my hand before gesturing to a cushioned armchair in front of his desk. In spite of his age, his spine was as straight as mine and he shook my hand firmly. I almost believed he was genuinely appreciative of my efforts, as though he wasn't paying the firm copious amounts for any of us to be anywhere he wanted.

I conducted the meeting like an informal presentation, recapping the steps our team had taken over the past year, the areas we had focused on, and the areas I recommended reviewing more closely in the coming year. By the time I'd finished, I could tell he was impressed.

"So you're saying your AI tool can flag emails by employees who have stolen from the company, even though the email doesn't directly mention anything nefarious?" he asked, latching onto one of the features I'd covered last. I smiled. Clients were always interested in hearing about that one.

"It calculates the emotion and picks up on trends in emails. So it might, for example, recognize a veiled threat, or flag an employee whose emails are consistently charged with negative emotions."

"Is that really effective in catching fraud?" In spite of the doubt in his voice, I had his attention.

"Maybe not by itself," I said. "And it's relatively new to our company, so we haven't been using it long enough to know how much of a difference it makes. But it definitely reports some interesting trends. We've actually had HR departments requesting to use it to ascertain employee satisfaction levels." I laughed a little at that. "It would offer a pretty limited picture though. For now, we're using it as a tool to tell us where to look."

"I see," Mr. Worthing said. He rubbed his chin. "Do you think it would be useful for us?"

"We can give it a try," I answered. "Although, we are also starting to use a more targeted screening tool that might be more useful for your organization. There's a common scam you're probably familiar with; it's been around for pretty much as long as email has existed. It happens when hackers are able to get access to the email account of someone important in the organization. They then send phishing emails out to other employees that appear to be from that leader requesting sensitive information. Someone in your internal accounting department might get an email that appears to be from the CFO, for example, asking for account numbers."

He nodded. "Sure, we've seen that attempted here."

"Well, we have this tool that can be used to screen all emails from a specific person; usually, we set it up for someone like you or your CFO, maybe your heads of HR and IT. It takes the tool a week to a month, depending on how many emails you send out, to get to know you, so to speak. Once it does, it can identify when an email that comes from your account is fraudulent, even if the sender attempts to copy your choice of words, email signature, and so on. The AI knows it's not you, and stops it from going through until you review it. Some of the product tests have found it to be better at detecting whether an email is genuine or not than decades-long coworkers, close friends, even family."

"Really?" he asked, eyebrows raised in surprise.

I nodded. "Humans are easier to fool," I said with a shrug, pushing away the unwanted image that sprang to my mind as I said it—Michael's face staring up at me. Innocent. Unbruised.

What if I just didn't hit him as hard as I thought?

"Some interesting stuff today, Ms. Brookes," Mr. Worthing said, pulling me from my thoughts. "I'll be in touch."

By the time I finally left his building, dropping my facade of confidence felt like shedding a heavy suit. I scolded myself for letting him get to me, for still feeling like an imposter after so many years of hard work. For allowing myself to feel small.

***

Ivy and I had plans to have lunch together that day, something we did at least a couple times a month. The first time I had asked her if she wanted to do lunch, the words formed awkwardly in my mouth, like a child repeating things I'd heard grown-ups say. She had laughed, thoroughly delighted.

"Do lunch?" she asked, "Is that something we do now? Oh, shit, are we the kind of people who 'do' lunch?"

Growing up, eating even fast-food takeout had been such a rare occasion that I could probably count the occurrences on one hand. I didn't eat at a sit-down restaurant for the first time until I was an adult.

I blushed when she laughed at me, but didn't mind it. Ivy was the only person I knew who always laughed like you were every bit as in on the joke as she was.

"Sure," I said shyly. "Why not?"

"Yes. Why the hell not?" And the simple tradition was born.

After I caught her up on the latest of my nighttime adventures, including the hair-pulling from the night before, she stared at me thoughtfully.

"All right, so it can't be Michael doing it in his sleep if he didn't go to bed at all last night, right?"

I shook my head. "I guess not. And going by what Michael says, it's happened mostly on nights like that; when he stayed up later than me or pulled all-nighters."

"You *only* have the dreams when Michael's not in bed with you?"

That felt a little like I was being cross-examined. "No, not only. The first dream, he was in bed with me when that happened. I don't know about all of them. Sometimes I don't wake up fully and check the time. And I don't always check with Michael to compare. I already sound like a crazy person demanding almost daily to know what time he went to bed the night before."

"How weird," Ivy said, not seeming to know what else to say. "Are you stressed about anything in particular?"

"I don't feel like I am."

"Okay, don't laugh, but are you eating right before bed?"

I looked at her blankly. "What?"

"I know it might sound kooky to you, but going to bed on a full stomach can fuck up your sleep. And I've read that even eating the wrong kinds of things can cause nightmares. Dairy, spicy foods, that kinda thing." She laughed at the look on my face. "Okay! I'm not sure if the type of food matters. But avoiding food right before bed has always been good advice anyway, damnit. And don't knock it; the food and things we put into our bodies affect us a lot more than we realize."

It was a common theme for her. Whole-body wellness. "All right, Dr. Ivy. I'll cut down on my evening snacks. It's not like I was sipping milk and munching on jalapeños before bed anyway, but okay."

She looked gratified. "You're for sure nothing's bothering you about Michael?" she asked.

"Everything is going really well," I said. I met her eyes and smiled to reassure her. The simple statement that things were well had a layered meaning for us. Our childhood had been bare, with a mother who was plagued by a spectrum of anxiety disorders and had hardly left her home for the last ten years of her life. She was paranoid that everyone from the cashier at our local grocery store to distant family members and neighbors we didn't know might have plans to do us harm. She talked to people who weren't there, sometimes an agitated, unceasing stream of muttering Ivy and I could hear from the living room as she paced around her bedroom for hours.

On top of everything with our mother, my father had struggled with severe depression and killed himself when I was barely old enough to remember him. Ivy's father had been in and out of our lives for much of our childhood until he finally gave up, unable to deal with our mother's worsening state. For us, everything going well was an unexpected relief.

"Good," Ivy said. "Then try the food thing. And maybe start doing some yoga before bed. Are you still doing yoga?"

"Every now and then," I said, not wanting to admit it had been weeks. Ivy was a firm believer in the benefits of yoga, but my workdays including commute were at least nine hours and could get up to twelve. When I worked out, I wanted maximum efficiency, which usually meant running.

The whole time I told Ivy about my dreams, I found myself wanting to defend Michael and clarify that I was confident now that none of it had actually happened, that he was telling the truth. But Ivy didn't raise the possibility in the first place. It didn't seem to occur to her that Michael could be messing with my head and lying to me.

After we finished lunch and I headed back to the office, I kept thinking about her lack of suspicion.

What's wrong with me? Why am I so quick to jump to something so awful?

Michael and I had been together for years. He was the least manipulative person I'd ever met; he couldn't hide his motives if his deepest desires depended on it.

***

When I got home that evening, Michael was in the kitchen.

"How was your big meeting?" he asked, referring to Mr. Worthing. I was surprised he remembered.

"It was good," I said. "He seemed happy with everything I shared with him."

"That's great. How was the rest of your day?"

"Fine. I had lunch with Ivy. She's doing great, and the bookshop is finally starting to take off."

"Did she offer you a cut?"

I flinched, but Michael didn't catch it. Ivy used the money from our mother's insurance policy, money that was designated to be split between us, to open the bookshop. I had insisted she take all of it. Michael didn't seem to notice the irritation in my voice as I answered, "No, and I would never take it."

"Even if she started making millions?" He was being facetious, but it wasn't the first time he had mentioned it.

"It's an independent secondhand bookshop. Probably the most she can hope for is to cover expenses and have enough to live on. And she deserved to get all the money. She cared for Mom for years while I ran off to college, and all the money that was left after funeral expenses was barely enough to get the place started. She doesn't owe me anything. It was the right thing to do." The words poured out in a torrent, and Michael's hands were in the air before I finished talking.

"I'm joking, just joking. I know you wouldn't take it. I'm glad she's doing so much better."

"She's been better for several years now," I said, my words clipped and short. Sometimes he acted like she was some crazy family member. The biggest drama in his family over the past decade seemed to be whether Elliot would major in art or business.

"She had a few bad years," I said, "with good reason. She's been responsible and stable most of her life. Let it go."

"I said I'm glad everything is better," he said. "I wasn't trying to imply anything."

I met his gaze. He was staring at me curiously, questioningly, as if my defense of my sister was abnormal. I softened and tried to let my frustration go. "I know," I said. "Everything is good."

Saying it for the second time that day somehow made it feel less true.

CHAPTER SEVEN

MY MOTHER DIED about a year after I graduated from college. Sudden cardiac failure. I learned afterward that it's common in people with mental health problems like hers, especially when they aren't careful about what pills they take or what they mix them with.

At the time, I had my first real job at a professional firm, and I had been dating Michael for a couple of months. The week of her funeral, I went back to our depressing little house where Ivy still lived, one of only a handful of times I'd visited since I'd left for college. I parked my rental in the street and made my way to the front door, relieved to think it might be the last time I'd ever have to see it.

I went in without knocking since Ivy had texted that she might be in the backyard and not hear my knock. It had once been my front door too, but I felt like an intruder walking through it that day. That feeling fell away as I glanced around the familiar living room, still my childhood home, barely changed. The same ancient brown couch was pushed against the wall farthest from the door, across the small room that could be traversed in five steps. The same yellowed, peeling linoleum marked the shift from the living room to the kitchen to my right. The same battered wooden table with only three chairs filled the extra kitchen space. I couldn't remember ever needing a fourth.

My feeling of intrusion had barely fled when another took its place with a jolt. Ivy came in from the backyard to greet me, and I froze at the sight of her. She looked ill. She was gaunt and colorless, and her hands were trembling. Her makeup was badly done, calling attention to rather than distracting from her blotchy complexion. Her clothes hung loosely from her shoulders. It had been less than a year since I'd seen her last.

How could she have changed this much?

I blinked away my shock and embraced her quickly, wondering at the idea that she could be responding to our mother's death so extremely. My guilt rose; I was usually filled with guilt when I thought of Ivy trapped in that house, refusing to allow me to share the same fate or any portion of it, but new guilt filled me in that moment. I had almost expected to see relief in Ivy, relief at finally being free to build a life of her own. I came prepared to reassure her that it was okay to feel that way. Instead, I was seeing Ivy's grief so clearly etched across her face, surpassing anything I had expected. Anything I was feeling myself. My own grief was as much for everything our mother wasn't and had never been as it was for anything we had lost.

How could she be this selfless?

Our mother had not been a kind woman. Maybe she was, once—I remembered getting to lick the spoon when she was baking brownies. Ivy got the bowl, but our mom always left extra batter on the spoon to even it out. I remembered trips to the library and getting to pick any book I wanted from a certain section, and never being told to hurry even though I tried to look at every single one. And I grieved heavily for that version of my mother. But she had been drinking for years by the time I was a teenager, and mixing in whatever pills she could get her hands on. Her anxiety and paranoia grew while she refused any treatment or advice that required leaving the house or making changes. She could be cruel and seemed to have little kindness or gratitude to spare for Ivy.

I had arrived as quickly as I could after Ivy called to give me the news, intending to help her make funeral plans, but as soon as we hugged and sat down together, she began to go through the plans. Already made.

"The funeral is Saturday. The ceremony will be real small, of course; we'll have a headstone next to her mom. We're not doing anything afterward, I don't think. There aren't a whole lot of people coming, you know?"

"Thank you for taking care of everything," I said meekly as we sat together. Useless and empty. "I'm sorry it's all fallen on you. I'm sorry it's always fallen on you." My voice trailed away, the words sounding as meaningless as they always did.

She looked like she wanted to say something, words swimming around behind her lips but unable to break the surface.

I wondered if she was angry with me for not having been around more, or if she could tell I wasn't as sad as she was. I wanted to ask, but was too afraid she would tell me how awful I was. I waited in tense silence.

"I think," Ivy finally began, "I think that if it took any longer than this for her to die, that it might have been me in that grave."

I whirled to look at her and was surprised to see that rather than grief, Ivy's face was contorted by something that looked like shame.

"What do you mean?" I asked.

"I've been a mess, Jana," she said, her voice hard. "I've had no future and I've used that as an excuse to fuck up any future I could have."

"What do you mean?" I asked again, dumbly.

"Jana, I'm fucked up. I'm always fucked up. These past few months when Mom's health got so bad. I've let everything go. But I can't blame it all on that. I've been a mess for years." Her voice cracked and she dropped her face into her hands.

As soon as she said it, I couldn't believe I hadn't seen it before. Every time I'd visited, there were celebratory drinks at every meal. The last time I was there, she made drinks with breakfast—*"It's like a vacation having you over, you know,"* she'd said.

"What about now?" I asked, scared of the answer.

"I want to stop," she said, to my relief. "I want to do better. But I don't know if I can. It's got to the point that it's all I've been doing, and I don't know how to start trying to have a life without it, without her."

"Ivy, I'm so sorry I wasn't here. I wish you had told me it was so bad, I wish I had helped more."

"There's nothing you could've done, it's not about that. I'm not trying to make you feel bad. You didn't make me stay here." She chewed her lip. "I felt so trapped, and I started feeling like if I'd be stuck here with her anyway, what did it matter?"

"You have all the time in the world to have a future now," I said quickly, wanting her to agree to be better, wanting her to be okay. "I'll help you. I know I owe you everything."

"You don't owe me. There was never any reason for you to stay, too. Sometimes knowing you were doing better was the only thing that kept me going at all, kept me from going too far."

From that day, we'd been closer than ever. She returned to St.

Louis with me, selling our childhood home for next to nothing just to be rid of it. We both wanted to do better, to have more from life than our parents had managed to take. Ivy started her business and the healthy glow that adorned her face, now rounded and smooth, was a consistent reassurance to me that we had done it. After everything we went through, we were happy.

Chapter Eight

MY EYES FLEW open and Michael's face was all I saw, an inch from my own. We had each stirred in our sleep toward the middle of the bed where the edges of our pillows met, and we came to rest facing each other, nose to nose, the tips almost touching.

The sight jolted me awake and I froze in place, staring wide-eyed at the face before me. It was so dark I could barely make out the outline of his familiar features. In spite of his nearness, I couldn't even tell if his eyes were open. Was he intentionally this close to me, staring at me, trying to frighten me?

An old fear of mine reached up from childhood, the idea of someone unseen staring at me from the darkness.

Would he burst out laughing the moment I softly called his name or touched his face, if I shifted away from him or reached for the light?

Would he make a sudden noise or grab my wrist?

There was a face he sometimes made when he stared at me while I wasn't paying attention. He would lock his eyes on me, wide and unblinking, with a frozen, unnatural smile plastered on his face, until I finally noticed him looking. Then he'd laugh because it never failed to startle me.

Was he smiling now?

Was he making that face, frozen and unnatural?

My eyes strained in the blackness, unblinking, fixed on the blank, shadowy circles where I knew his eyes to be.

Were they open?

The moments crawled by as my eyes raked over his face, trying desperately to discern whether he was staring back at me.

And what if he is? What if he is messing with me? What is there to be frightened of in that?

But then, nobody likes to be startled, however harmless it is.

If he was sleeping, what would happen if he woke to see me staring at him, pale and frightened? I forced myself to blink and relax my intense gaze. I exhaled silently and pushed myself away from him ever so slightly.

He didn't stir.

I moved further away, newly aware of aching muscles that complained of time spent rigid, unmoving, unbreathing. I raised myself onto my elbow and from that angle, I could finally see his peaceful, sleeping face, with all the innocence of eyes that remained closed, and I smiled in the darkness at my foolishness. I was relieved he hadn't woken up, leaving no witness to my suspicions and my strange behavior. I laid back down, drained and exhausted, and curled against him contentedly, loving him more for having thought badly of him, and began drifting back to sleep.

"Are you scared of me?" his voice sounded in the darkness, and my eyes flew open again. This time, I reached for the lamp so fast I almost knocked it over as I flipped it on, panic rising in my chest. A scream was lodged in my throat, ready for release at the slightest indication that another person was in the room with us.

But it was empty.

Michael was sleeping and still next to me.

I stared at him suspiciously and nudged him, but his mouth hung slightly open and his body was limp. My eyes traveled around the room, searching, but there was nothing.

I must have started dreaming as I fell asleep.

I told myself that my mind, influenced by my paranoia, dreamed of Michael waking up and taunting me.

I couldn't think of another answer.

CHAPTER NINE

THE TENSION HAD to come to a head eventually. Michael didn't see it there, but it was; little bubbles of confusion and worry in my brain, waiting to burst. His hands, always his hands, all over me in the dark, innocent in the light. His voice, whispering to me in the night, quietly in my ear while I slept, loud and careless in the day.

I was deep asleep one night when his arm wrapped tightly around my ribs.

My eyes fluttered open; it was barely after midnight.

Like the other times, he began running his hands possessively over me, squeezing and rubbing. I frowned, wanting nothing more than to ignore him and stay asleep. But a whisper in the back of my mind harassed me, pleading for me to wake. Something was wrong.

His hand went to my breast and massaged it forcefully. I was still half asleep, my mind groggy, trying to comprehend what was happening.

He will stop if I ignore him.

Then his hand descended and slipped between my legs and grabbed me. Hard.

I yelped, finally wide awake, and leapt out of bed.

I yelled at him from the foot of the bed, standing over him. "You can't grab me like that! Do you have any idea what it's like to be woken up like that?" Tears of anger and exhaustion burned in my eyes. "Now I finally know! I know you've been waking me up and messing with me and lying to my face!"

Questions stormed through my mind. How could he lie to me? How could he think any of it was okay? And why, what was he trying to do to me?

My worst suspicions, confirmed. Michael had been lying to me and making me feel ridiculous, in addition to completely disregarding any shred of boundaries I had. I stomped away, too tired and confused and hurt to say anything more. All the other times, when he had laughed at me and teased, convinced me I was dreaming, pretended he hadn't been in bed at all, it was him. It was really him. I was enraged and I was vindicated, finally knowing it wasn't my own mind at fault.

I used the bathroom and stared at myself in the mirror afterwards, taking consolation in the confirmation that I was awake, aware, not dreaming. I was boiling with disbelief that he could play with my mind so callously.

Flushed and vibrating with anger, I went out into the hallway and lowered the heat to sixty-eight degrees. I considered sleeping in the guest room, but the bed wasn't made up and I didn't want anything else that would make me miss more sleep. The living room couch was an even worse option since Holly took anyone lying on the couch as an invitation to act as a weighted blanket. I decided to go back to bed; if anyone should leave, it was him.

I returned to the dark, silent bedroom and lay down, feeling all the unshakeable self-assurance of someone who is right blending miserably with the turmoil of not knowing what that meant for my marriage. But I had begun to question my ability to tell realistic dreams from reality, and once the question was gone, the enormous strain it had been putting on me was lifted. I finally knew I was not the problem.

Paranoid. Twisted. Confused. Unbalanced. Disturbed.

Those harsh words and more had been floating around in my mind after each strange dream, each assurance from Michael that he hadn't touched me, hadn't talked to me, hadn't done anything to me while I slept.

My relief that I wasn't completely crazy was almost enough to overshadow the sadness beginning to build, burning in the back of my eyes and in the pit of my stomach, that the man sleeping next to me might not be who I thought I married.

"The man I thought I married" isn't a phrase I ever thought I'd use. We dated for years before we got engaged. We met volunteering for a nearby state park. One of the first interactions we ever had was when I asked him how long he'd been volunteering and he said, "Ever since I was nineteen." And when he saw that I looked impressed, he quickly followed up with, "I was a moron and it was court-ordered after I got cited for underage drinking. I just never stopped." He grinned at me and added, "Volunteering, that is. Though I guess I never fully stopped drinking either, when it comes down to it. Just stopped being a minor."

He was always so honest.

My back to him, at least a foot of space between us, I went back to sleep.

I left for work early the next morning, not bothering to wake him, and I didn't speak to him all day. I checked my phone repeatedly, expecting an apology, but not getting any.

I wondered if he felt awkward and guilty and was too ashamed to try and make it right in a text, a thought that gave me some satisfaction. Multiple times throughout the day I began typing out a message to Ivy to tell her what had happened, only to erase it and put my phone aside.

I couldn't put this in a text.

I considered calling her or stopping by when I left work. Yet when I imagined explaining what had happened, I thought of the awkwardness of saying it all, and my cheeks burned.

He grabbed me.

Grabbed you where?

I couldn't.

I was ashamed of Michael, ashamed of his behavior, ashamed of my own blindness. I spent the entire day distracted and inefficient, staring at my work without understanding it, attending meetings and group calls and barely knowing what the subject had been when they ended. When five o'clock finally arrived, I was tempted to stay late and not message him, let him worry and wonder until he finally broke and called me. But I'd already been useless enough. There was no need to add any more time at the office in that state.

The days had been growing shorter as we headed deeper into autumn, and darkness was already falling by the time I arrived home. I steeled myself at the door. I couldn't consider everything the impending conversation would mean for our relationship. I kept shoving those thoughts aside. My focus was narrow. I wanted him to know I knew that it was him, that it was him every time. That I wasn't crazy.

I wanted him to acknowledge his actions.

I wanted an apology and an explanation. Whatever that meant for us.

The house was dim when I entered; Michael was in the habit of turning off any lights he wasn't using.

Always so responsible.

I stood in the entryway for a moment, half expecting him to greet me with some token of apology. Flowers or cookies, or something. But I was met with silence. I stared down the long hall that led to our bedroom and saw only darkness. The kitchen and dining area to my left was dark as well. He hadn't even bothered to start dinner.

No apology, then.

I thought at least there'd be pasta.

His office was where I usually found him, and apparently, tonight would be no different.

I could see the dim light coming from under his door as I began to climb the stairs. My fingers went to my hair to twist it nervously and I forced them down, clenching my hands and digging my nails into my palms instead.

What is he going to say?

I wondered if he would try to turn it around somehow. There was no way he could have slept through it, but maybe he would downplay the importance, say I was overreacting. I took a deep breath and opened the door to see him sitting at his computer, absorbed in his work. He looked up and smiled when I came in. Holly stayed where she was, tucked under his desk, only lifting her head lethargically and dropping it again.

"How was work?" He asked it casually.

"Fine," I answered. I stared at him, waiting and expecting him to say something, to apologize, to launch into an explanation, anything.

"Is everything okay?" he asked absently, his eyes already back on his computer.

How could he be so infuriating?

But I remained standing where I was, on the other side of the small room. "After last night, no," I said.

"What happened?" he asked, barely glancing up again.

I stared at him dumbfounded. He was going to make me spell it out.

"Why would you grab me like that while I was sleeping?" I

didn't try to keep the rage out of my voice anymore. "And how could you lie to me about it all those other times?"

Now he looked up and fixed me with his stare.

"Grab you like what?" He asked it slowly, his voice measured.

Could he possibly think it was an innocent caress? Could his perception of the situation be so drastically different? Or was he still pretending it hadn't happened?

I wavered for a moment, but I knew I had every right to be upset.

"I yelled at you for it," I said. "Are you saying you don't remember?" Sleepwalking began to seem like a possibility again.

"You did not yell at me," he said. His voice was flat and began to take an impatient edge.

The little restraint I had maintained left me then. "This isn't funny," I snapped. "Stop messing with my head!"

"I am not messing with your head! Last night I came to bed, I had my arm around you for maybe five minutes, then I rolled over and went to sleep. That was it. No yelling, no grabbing. Nothing else happened."

"No!" I was shouting now, and Holly jumped to her feet and whined. "You came to bed, you wrapped your arm around me, and you squeezed tightly. I pulled on your arm to loosen your grip because it was uncomfortable and you were waking me up, and you started rubbing me all over. Then you moved your hand between my legs and grabbed me! You grabbed me really hard." My voice began to break, the last sentence falling into a pathetic whine, and I hated that he was making me cry, hated him for making me say it all out loud. But I pressed on. "I shoved you away and I got up and yelled at you. I went to the bathroom, went out into the hallway and turned down the temperature, and came back to bed."

Michael had risen to his feet during my heated account and he stood before me, exasperation and disbelief mingling on his face.

"*None* of that happened," he said. "Stop fucking blaming me for your weird fucking dreams!"

Michael had never sworn at me like that, yelling in my face.

His words were like a spell that snapped me out of any confidence I had. The moment he said it, my certainty became less certain. Doubt descended like a sudden fog over the memories that had been so clear a moment before. They faded and became dreamlike in my mind, leaving me with a layer of lingering fear and an acute sense of foolishness.

Once more faced with doubt, I suddenly knew how strange it was that he hadn't responded when I yelled at him. How could he just lie there? Not defending himself, not apologizing. How had that not occurred to me earlier?

I realized with a start that I couldn't remember seeing his face during the incident at all, only his figure in the darkness, buried in the blankets. He didn't look at me when I shouted or when I came back to bed.

"What time did you come to bed?" I asked, grasping for something, anything, that would put me on solid ground again.

"Around two a.m.," he answered evenly. I could see the slight shade of victory cross his face as he read in mine that that wasn't the answer I was looking for. "I didn't even step foot downstairs from the time you went to bed until I joined you at two. I wasn't asleep, and I wasn't anywhere near you." Another point against sleepwalking.

I had one last card to play, one last trail to follow. "What's the AC set to?" I tried to ask the question with demanding certainty, more like a statement than a question, a statement that would undoubtedly prove my point, but my voice wavered against my will.

His eyes narrowed, but he walked deliberately down the stairs, through the living room, and down the hall toward our bedroom, grudgingly humoring me as I trailed behind him.

"Seventy degrees," he said, standing next to the thermostat for me to see.

It didn't prove anything irrefutably, of course. I could imagine that he knew what the temperature was before we went to bed, even though I was the one who set it, who always set it, and I could imagine that he knew how much I had lowered it and then raised it again to thwart me. I could also imagine how insane I would sound if I said any of that out loud. It was enough, combined with everything else, to make me believe him.

And I was crushed. I had never felt so foolish in my entire life.
Paranoid.
Twisted.
Confused.
Unbalanced.
Disturbed.
"I can't believe it was another dream . . ." I stammered. "It was

so real. I remember getting up out of bed and going to the bathroom and coming out into the hallway . . . It was so real."

He softened and stopped looking angry with me, to my relief. Now that he wasn't being accused of anything, he could even muster a halfway reassuring smile about it. He took a deep breath and let it out in a rush, and I realized how stressed he was by the argument, and guilt was added to the churning ball of anxiety forming a knot deep in my gut.

"Well, I think we need drinks," he said abruptly, brushing past me in the hall and walking toward the kitchen, leaving me to follow meekly behind.

He poured gin into a tumbler in swift, deft motions. "Are you getting enough sleep?" he asked after he finished shaking. Michael was in problem-solving mode.

"Not really," I said. "I mean, these dreams or whatever they are keep waking me up."

"Have you been reading any horror stories before bed or watching any scary shows?" He dumped olives unceremoniously into the glasses, handed me a martini, and took a sip of his own.

Watching the wrong thing, eating the wrong thing, doing the wrong exercise at the wrong time, thinking the wrong things about my spouse. Everyone seemed to think it was all because I was doing something wrong.

"You know I hate horror," I said. "The scariest thing I've read all year was a history book about World War II, and I couldn't finish it." *Tell him. It's time.* My heart slammed against my chest as I considered forming the words, telling him everything.

A pause before the next question. "Is something bothering you about us?" he asked.

Us. I don't know when it happens but that word grows in a relationship until it means so many things: our marriage, our life together, our history, our future, our happiness, our goals, our love. It stands for everything.

I knew that question was the question he had wanted to ask, the one he thought about as he asked the others, the one that played white noise in his ears so that he barely heard my answers until that question.

I suddenly needed to laugh, needed him to laugh, needed to be the one who made him laugh; I am ashamed to admit how much I needed it, but in that moment, I needed desperately to know he still thought well of me, that he wasn't questioning my mental or emotional strength, that he wasn't repulsed by my fears and accusations, that he still valued me, respected me, wanted me.

I stepped around the counter that divided us and wrapped my arms around his waist, laying my head against his chest, conscious of the stiffness with which his arms encircled me.

"No," I said. "Everything is better than I hoped it would be." His arms began to relax around me. "I think the first dream I had, about you standing in the doorway watching me, scared me more than I realized. I started thinking about it every night without noticing I was doing it. Something that wasn't you, standing in the doorway, coming into our bedroom." It wasn't until I said it out loud that I realized how much that figure had been present in my mind. "And without realizing it," I continued, "I guess I started having more and more dreams about someone . . . pretending to be you." Michael looked appeased, the assurances making him relax even while they formed a shadow in my own mind. I was unsettled by the idea, disturbed by my own explanation.

Something pretending to be you.

Tell him now, now is the time to tell him you fucking coward.

But I didn't.

Dr. Goulding, a therapist I had seen briefly after my mom died, popped into my head, and I wondered if I should make an appointment even while hoping desperately that Michael wouldn't suggest it. I waited in tense anticipation. I had only seen her to be safe, to make sure I didn't have my mother's problems. Michael had never really understood the need for me to see a therapist when I wasn't having problems, and if he suddenly thought I needed her it would have crushed me.

The suggestion didn't come, and I let out a breath.

The memory of the night before played over and over in my mind even as he held me and kissed me, reassuring me that he wasn't upset anymore. When I thought of the night before, I could feel every touch, I could hear the sound of my own voice raised in anger, the rage and indignation that flooded my body; I could retrace every footstep in my mind, from the bed to the bathroom to the hallway and back to bed. And a lingering unease stayed floating in my mind.

I stopped telling him about my dreams after that.

PART TWO

Chapter Ten

BY THE TIME Michael's parents arrived a few days later, things had more or less returned to normal.

Michael's mother Lucy was everything I'd ever thought of as mom-like. She called everybody 'love' and she brushed away handshakes with hugs, hugs she meant and finished with an extra squeeze every time. She was the most sympathetic listener anyone could hope for, whether you needed serious advice or wanted to complain about someone who was rude. She made the best pancakes I'd ever tasted and she put real butter in everything she cooked.

She greeted us with exclamations—"Oh, Jana, you cut your hair, it's darling on you, love!"—and tight embraces that lasted not a fraction less than four full seconds. Last second: squeeze.

"Oh, is this a new picture of you two and Holly? It's such a good picture!" She gestured to the frame hung in the entryway.

"Yes, we had a copy printed for you, too," I said, my voice drowned in the next exclamation.

"Oh, and here's Holly!" She bent to ruffle her ears. "She's putting on weight! She's lost her puppy metabolism, hasn't she?"

Michael's and his father's voices bounced through the small space simultaneously.

"Hi, hi, hi!" Doug's booming greeting filled the entrance along with his big, rustling coat, thick scarf, and heavy boots—all adding to his already large frame of over six feet. Doug had begun wearing his beard long and thick in recent years and he had a problem with one of his knees, which gave him a swaying gait that seemed to put him at once to my right and left. While he wasn't as fit as he'd once been, he wasn't significantly overweight either. He used big gestures and sweeping movements, and everything about him seemed designed to fill the space with energy, usually cheerful.

Adding to his bulk were several packages and Lucy's voice chimed in with, "We brought gifts, love! I know it's early, but since you said you weren't sure about coming down for Christmas yet, we just thought—"

"How are you, how are you, how are you?" Doug broke in alongside Lucy's explanations. A greeting for me, a greeting for Michael, a greeting for Holly. "Jana, you are a fine wine, every time I see you, you've gotten lovelier."

I thanked him, knowing how many times it was likely he had repeated those words, but grinning at hearing them in spite of myself.

Maybe it was the contrast of my own quiet childhood with so many afternoons Ivy and I spent in hushed voices and subdued play so we wouldn't disturb our mother while she rested, but it seemed to me that Michael's parents always seemed to arrive in a flurry fit for a group of at least ten cousins, aunts, uncles, and grandparents.

Dads saying dad cliches, moms giving mom hugs, parents doing parent things. My mind wandering uncontrolled at night into dark and hazy realms was nothing but another dirty secret to add to the pile, and it had no place in this world of pretend normal.

Maybe everyone's pretending, I mused hopefully.

"Let's put your things in the guest room," I said, when I had the chance, and despite having lived in the house for a year those words still felt strange on my tongue. Guest room. I had shared a twin bed with Ivy until we were teenagers and then we took turns getting to sleep in the bed for a week at a time while the other slept on the living room couch. One week in bed, one week on the couch; wash, rinse, hang to dry, and repeat. But there I was with a guest room in my house and two extra bedrooms upstairs that we didn't even use as bedrooms.

Sometimes it still felt like I was only impersonating a nice person with a nice family and a nice home.

We navigated down the hall to the spare bedroom, Michael's father managing to brush against both sides of the hallway in turn, bringing one picture nearly crashing to the floor if it hadn't caught against Lucy's hip close behind.

"Oh! My ass saved it," she said with a loud laugh, "I knew I ate those extra cookies for a reason!" She passed it nimbly back to Michael, who was bringing up the tail of our group with two of their bags, and he dropped them for a moment to put the picture safely back in its place.

I had moved to St. Louis for college because it had one of the schools I liked and was far enough from home to satisfy me, but Michael and his family were from the area originally. That evening, we picked up barbeque (*"We have to have barbeque while we're here, love, it's just not the same in Florida, you know!"*) and brought it home to eat.

"How's your job going, love?" Lucy asked me once we were all settled on the back porch with St. Louis-style ribs, brisket, potato salad, and baked beans spread out on the patio table. "Michael mentioned you got a promotion recently?"

"Yes," I said. "To senior manager."

"Oh, that was fast, wasn't it? Didn't you just start there?"

"A year ago, but I had experience and it was something we discussed going in. They rarely hire someone from the outside to manage a team, but based on my experience, they agreed to do a six-month evaluation and decide at that point. And I got it."

"What's next? Partner?" She smiled broadly.

"There are still a few steps before that," I said, smiling modestly.

Making partner, signing thirty-year mortgages, trading in the three-year-old vehicle because the warranty's gone and run out. I could forget it in our day-to-day lives, but having Lucy and Doug smiling at us like some vision of our potential future selves made it surreal again, how my life was turning out.

"And what about your sister?" Lucy asked "How's Ivy?"

"She's great."

"Doesn't she own a bookshop?" Doug asked. "We should go by tomorrow. Isn't it near the museum we're going to visit? I always like going to bookshops."

"Oh, that's a good idea, love. Let's do that."

They had met Ivy before, and I tried to push away the feeling of being caught between colliding worlds. "She would love that," I said.

After we finished our meal, we moved from the wooden picnic table Michael had built to the other side of the porch where there was a wicker couch and a swing. Michael and I took the swing, which had been weathered and gray when I discovered it in a pawn shop and was now painted white, while Lucy and Doug settled onto the couch.

The evening had been filled with updates on Michael's parents' home improvement projects, news of Michael's brother's new girlfriend who he was serious enough about that we'd be meeting her if we decided to come down for Christmas, and gossip about the people Michael and his parents both knew in St. Louis.

I was mostly quiet, listening to stories of people I didn't know, and I didn't mind the lack of pressure to participate, though I perked up when the topic turned.

"He's got the scaring competition going with her now," Lucy said of Michael's brother and the new girlfriend.

"Oh, no," Michael said. "Poor Abby."

"Poor Elliot," Doug corrected him. "Abby's got your talent for it. Elliot started it but just like with you, he can't give as good as he's getting."

"Oh, jeez. He never learns."

"What was it they were telling us this last visit?" Doug turned to Lucy. "She was waiting for him in the shower?"

"No, no, that's not right. He probably wouldn't mind that!" she giggled while Michael looked at me and rolled his eyes, embarrassed but smiling. "But no, she was standing outside the bathroom door with a mask while he showered. A clown mask or something. Exactly the kind of thing you used to do to him, Mikey. So mean."

I'd heard countless stories of Michael scaring Elliot when they were teenagers. Michael waking up an hour before Elliot so he could hide in the barn and lie in wait for Elliot to come out to do his chores. *He was so patient, love, that was the impressive part about the whole thing,* Lucy had said when she told the story.

Elliot hiding under their bed to scare Michael, but Michael spotting him and dropping to the floor with a scream, scaring Elliot so badly he hit his head on the bottom of the bed and ended up with a mild concussion. *Of course, I was angry at that one, but I couldn't blame Mikey fully since Elliot was the one trying to scare him.*

Michael cramming himself into the pantry closet to wait for Elliot to get a snack and accidentally getting Lucy instead. *He nearly gave me a heart attack, love. I banned scaring after that. They didn't listen, of course!*

There's no reason I should think anything of these stories now, I told myself.

"He never does that to you though, does he?" Lucy asked me.

"No," I said, but my voice came out hoarse from disuse and I cleared my throat quickly. "No," I said in a stronger voice and smiled. "He knows I would hate it."

"That's good," she said. "You call me if he starts acting up, love. I swear I thought he might give someone a heart attack when he was younger."

"Oh, I will," I said.

They certainly don't seem like the type of parents who'd raise a sociopath.

I was so startled by the thought that surfaced unbidden in my head that I flinched, and then looked around to see if anybody had noticed. No one looked at me strangely and the conversation continued flowing smoothly along, but Michael squeezed my hand slightly. I met his eyes and he was looking at me questioningly.

Did my hand jolt when I flinched? Can he tell what I'm thinking?

I smiled at him blandly. *Nothing at all, dear.*

***

The next day, the four of us made the trip to Ivy's bookshop as planned. She accepted Lucy's hug naturally, as though she expected it, and began chatting with them about books. I caught myself wondering if they thought her accent made her sound uneducated. I knew it was silly, especially when Lucy and Doug both had slight Midwestern accents themselves, and brushed the thought away. Ivy was as well-read as any bookstore owner would be expected to be, though I hoped she wouldn't swear too much while she talked to them.

Michael's dad enjoyed history and went straight for the nonfiction section, asking Ivy what she had on one war or another. Lucy wasn't much of a reader and wandered around the shop commenting on the furniture and decor.

Once Ivy had pointed Doug toward the sections he wanted and the rest of us had helped ourselves to coffee, though Ivy stuck with her usual herbal tea, Lucy gestured for Ivy to sit next to her to tell her about her business. I sat in a small loveseat across from them, and Michael chose the wooden chair between us.

Does he not want to sit next to me? I'd been watching him closely ever since our argument, looking for any sign at all that he was angry or worried, but he'd gone back to his usual self like the matter was resolved and didn't bear speaking of.

"Ivy, I'd love to hear all about what it took for you to get this bookshop started. Doug has talked about opening a business since we got married, I swear, but he never gets started. He loves woodworking you know, like Michael. He's the one who taught Michael a lot of it." She turned toward Michael. "Mikey, love, you are still making furniture, aren't you?"

"A little," Michael answered. "I don't make anything as impressive as Dad. A bench or a table is about as ambitious as I've gotten."

"Oh, well that's fine! It's still a good hobby to have. I'm glad you've stuck with it" She shifted her attention back to Ivy. "We have so many things that Doug's made over the years, you know;going back to our crib for the boys and the chair I used to rock them in."

"That's wonderful," Ivy said.

"We've had so many people ask about some of the things he's made that I thought maybe he should try selling some of it." She lowered her voice to a conspiratorial whisper, "Lord knows he makes more than we can use. There are only so many chairs I can fit in our house!"

Ivy began telling her about everything that went into opening her shop, from loans and real estate to city codes and marketing. She didn't seem offended that Lucy seemed to think starting a full-time business in a brick-and-mortar shop was the same as selling a piece of furniture once every few weeks, and I began to relax.

I knew it was silly to worry about them getting together.

Then, the moment the conversation hit a brief lull: "Did you tell them about the dreams?" Ivy asked out of nowhere.

Her words fell on the conversation like a gavel in the quiet room. Lucy raised her eyebrows in interest, while Doug looked up from the book he was scanning and moved closer to our conversation.

Oh god, I'm going to vomit. Where did that come from? Why would she bring it up? She might as well have punched me in the stomach. It wasn't like Ivy to be so careless, so imperceptive to my feelings. Michael's eyes met mine briefly, his expression inscrutable.

Did his jaw just tighten? If it did, is it because he doesn't like the topic or because he knows I don't?

"No, what dreams?" Lucy asked, smiling and looking around the circle as she waited for an answer.

I forced a smile. "I started having some weird dreams about Michael after we got married," I said. Ivy's smile had disappeared when she saw my strain and I reminded myself that I hadn't told her about the fight yet, that she never would have mentioned it if she knew the situation had begun creating tension between us.

"What kind of dreams?" Doug asked. Neither he nor Lucy seemed to pick up on my discomfort.

"Nothing major," I said, wishing Michael would chime in. "One night I dreamt he came to bed at four a.m., and I sat up and saw him standing in the doorway of our bedroom. Then when I asked him the next day why he came to bed so late, he said he was in bed around midnight."

"Oh, Michael, what are you doing to her?" Lucy laughed loudly as she asked the question, and Doug grinned. I cringed inwardly, thinking it might have been the worst possible reaction she could have had and wondering if Michael would be annoyed all over again at being accused.

Michael forced a smile back. "Nothing at all," he said.

"Was that the only dream?" Lucy asked.

Relief flooded me when Ivy stepped in before I had to think of a way to explain to my in-laws that I was having nightmares about their son groping me.

"When I first opened the shop and got my apartment down the street," she said, "I started having dreams of customers wandering into my bedroom with books they wanted to buy. They'd get mad about having to walk all that way in the middle of the night and ask why I wasn't around to help them. One woman told me she'd have to take her books and leave without paying. Crazy woman went on and on and on, lecturing me on how it was my own damn fault I wasn't getting paid."

Once she had everyone laughing, Michael and I both loosened up and he moved quietly from his chair to sit next to me on the loveseat. He took my hand and pressed it to his lips for a moment, then held it in his lap as Ivy continued. "There was one in particular that got to me. Getting this place up to code was an actual, living nightmare, so of course it only makes sense I'd have dreams about everything breakin' right and left. The plumbing in particular was a beast. One night, I dreamed the pipes in all the walls burst open and flooded the place, and of course since it was a dream, the water didn't go anywhere, out the windows or anything, just filled up the room slowly. Apparently, in my head this whole building is water tight. But for some reason I couldn't make myself leave. By the time I started moving toward the door, the water was up to my chest and books were floating everywhere and I couldn't get through it all. Point being, change makes your mind think of some crazy shit. Even if it's good change."

I was so relieved that she moved the topic away from us that I didn't even care about her swearing.

***

The rest of Lucy and Doug's visit passed without incident, at least from everyone else's perspectives. Part of me hoped something would happen; I imagined Doug asking Michael over coffee time, "Why were you pacing the hallway outside our bedroom door in the middle of the night?" Or Lucy mentioning with a laugh that she saw a man walking along the road in front of our house early in the day, before the sun was all the way up—a man who looked oddly familiar, though it was hard to tell through the morning mist that still clung to the ground.

But it seemed to be only me who saw and heard those things, and by then I was too afraid to ask if anyone else had.

Chapter Eleven

"YOU LOOK TIRED." Maria sat on the other side of my desk while we reviewed her reports, and her eyes met mine from beneath her jagged bangs. She had exchanged her chin-length curls for an edgy pixie cut within a month of starting her new job at the firm, and I marveled at her ability to flow through so many changes in rapid succession. New city, new job, new hair. She was proving herself quickly, not only learning the work easily but also speaking up in meetings and offering new ideas. She was opinionated and comfortable about sharing her thoughts.

I tried not to be bothered by it. I knew I was good at my job, but I'd once watched a video from the diversity and inclusion team in HR about why women get passed over for promotions and almost cried when the speaker talked about what she called "the silent workhorse type"—the worker who keeps her head down and does her work well and thinks that will be enough to earn recognition and promotions, but it isn't. The sense of not being enough hovered over me everywhere: my efforts to choose the right partner weren't enough to ensure a smooth marriage. Everything I'd done to get away from my mother and have a different life than hers wasn't enough to keep my mind safe from whatever demons had plagued her. Ever since the dreams started, a part of me was convinced it was only the beginning of a downward spiral, that I'd end up like her—bitter, broke, helpless, and alone—no matter what I did.

I tried to push the negative thoughts aside.

"I am tired," I admitted to Maria. "I kept waking up last night. I don't know why."

Of course I knew why. I'd had another confusing dream. I kept thinking I woke up because of footsteps on the second floor. The first time, I assumed it was Michael and I ignored it. The second time, I realized Michael was already in bed next to me. I wanted to shake him and ask if he heard the noise, but they faded away and eventually, after several minutes of silence, I faded away too. Finally, the third time, I woke up completely and found myself alone, and the noises were more distinct than ever. I didn't want to investigate by myself, so I stayed in bed and reached for my phone.

Is that you pacing? I messaged Michael.

Sorry, didn't know you could hear. I'll stop.

Thx. Were you in bed earlier?

No, but I'll be down soon. <3

Why had I thought someone was next to me the second time I'd woken up? Had I woken up at all?

Or was it yet another dream of him next to me?

After that, I kept falling back asleep and having shallow dreams where Michael was sleeping next to me one moment and gone the next. By the time he came to bed in the early hours of the morning, I had reached that tortuous stage of sleeplessness that had me counting the hours of sleep I had left if I managed to fall asleep immediately.

"I'm sorry," Maria was saying. "I'm a terrible insomniac. Now that I'm doing the whole eight-to-five thing, I'm trying really hard to go to bed at an adult human hour. But it's so hard."

I nodded like I could relate, even though I had maintained a consistent sleep schedule in college and rarely had trouble before the dreams started. I rallied and turned back to the spreadsheets on the monitors.

I had been showing Maria how to read the performance reports that showed her employee statistics, from error rates and client satisfaction scores to her average timelines and adherence to deadlines. Since she didn't have numbers in all the categories yet, I pulled up my own reports to demonstrate. All our scores were shared to the whole team; the firm said it was to increase accountability and provide opportunities for recognition, but I suspected they were more interested in cultivating a competitive environment that made us all afraid of slipping to the lower end of the rankings.

I tried not to look smug when Maria expressed surprise over my deadlines score. I hadn't missed a single one since I started.

"Believe it or not, that's not uncommon here," I said. "This firm has high standards."

Though it's not necessarily the norm to be this high, I didn't say. I was one of only a few people on the team who had scores that perfect. I continued going through the system with her, and it was a confidence boost I had needed.

I might be tired, and maybe I'm going crazy, but at least I'm still good at my job.

Chapter Twelve

I **COULDN'T SLEEP** again that night, but it wasn't because of dreams. After working most of the night before, Michael had collapsed into bed early and was letting out a continuous stream of loud, guttural snores. For all my complaints about him staying up too late, his falling asleep before me wasn't easy to cope with either.

I began to wonder if it would be crazy to go work on my table. Ivy's table, technically. The beautifully carved, solid wood table was waiting in the workshop, and the thought of working on it tickled the back of my mind. It felt like a strange thing to do at night, and I told myself I should stay put and read, or go watch television until I got tired, like a normal person.

But it wasn't very late, and I was off the next day. I had finished sanding the table earlier that evening, after stripping the old stain and filling in the dents, so it was waiting in the workshop, ready to be primed. I counted the hours in my head; if I primed it that night, the next day it would be ready to be painted. And I might even be able to do both coats of paint and the protective finish all before the weekend ended. My fingers tingled at the thought of starting the project, but still I hesitated.

It was dark. I would have to pull on my boots and go traipsing through the backyard to the workshop. And I'd be working out there alone. I wondered if it would be stupid, considering the man I'd seen and everything else that had been going on.

But just then, Michael let out a snore like a shout, loud enough to make me jump and almost yelp. That decided it. I could take Holly with me if I was really worried. I slid out of bed and crept out of our room, grabbing my boots and some sweatpants on my way out. When I reached the living room, I pulled the pants over my shorts, zipped a hoodie over my tank top, and stepped into my boots. It was a chilly night, and I stared doubtfully out the living room windows toward the workshop for a moment, questioning my zeal once more. The workshop wasn't far from the house, and the moon was bright enough that I could see across the grass until it met the woods behind our home, where the dark wall of trees extinguished any light. I turned on the back porch light, but its rays stretched only a few feet beyond the porch and made the rest of the yard darker by comparison. I glanced from the woods back to the workshop and at the sides of the yard where solid privacy fences towered.

I thought again of the fresh, clean, sanded wood and the satisfaction of dragging my paint brush over it, watching it turn into something new. Holly had risen from her place in the corner and moved like a shadow to sit next to me, her orange-brown eyes intent upon my face, her wolf-like features still and intent.

"Do you want to go outside?" I asked her softly. Her ears perked straight up and she stood at attention. Asking a dog if they want to go outside is as good as a promise, and she waited for me to follow through. "Well, if you think it's a good idea," I said, ruffling her ears.

I opened the back door and stepped into the chill night air. *This is silly. Who paints furniture at ten o'clock at night?* I stared reluctantly at the back yard. But then, which was crazier—working on a table at night or being frightened of the dark like a child, unable to step outside on your own property?

I walked purposefully toward the workshop, averting my eyes from the grove and trying not to imagine what might be lurking there in the pitch black of the woods. I hated that I allowed myself to be nervous in my own yard, but I couldn't stop myself from breaking into quick strides that were almost a run for the last few steps to the workshop. I sprang lightly up the steps, flipped on the light, and slammed the door behind myself and Holly in quick, successive motions.

It was warmer in there, shielded from the windy night, and it was bathed in familiar shades of browns and yellows; filled with comforting scents of paint, stain, lumber, and dust. I let out my breath in relief. The table was sitting in the middle of the workshop on a sheet of canvas. The remnants of Michael's last project were stowed neatly away, all the tools and furniture I wouldn't need pressed against the walls. I had already carefully cleaned the table of dust earlier that day and laid out all the supplies I would need.

There was one window in the workshop, on the back wall farthest from the house, looking out at the woods. I cracked it for ventilation; it was a windy enough night that even a couple of inches kept fresh air circulating, then I turned from the window to face the table.

I took off my boots and put them on the stool against the wall with everything else, and lowered myself to sit cross-legged on the floor in front of the table. Immediately, I rose to my feet again. The mental image of the window staring at me from behind had sent a prickling sensation down my neck. I moved to the other side of the workshop and sat back down, facing the window. As I reached for the flathead screwdriver and began prying open the can of primer, I couldn't stop glancing at the blank, black window, peering out into blind darkness. It wasn't much better than having my back to it.

I wondered if I would be able to tell if someone stood out there, staring at me, their face inches from the glass. How close could they be without me knowing it?

Trying to pretend it wasn't Michael's face I imagined there, I bent to my work. I quickly became absorbed in the task. I took my time, taking extra care on the trickier areas like the ornately carved legs. I was gratified each time I ran my brush over an area that had been especially scarred, pleased to see the last evidence of my patching and sanding and scraping disappear completely under the white primer.

The whole table took me over an hour, and a thrill of pleasure ran through me at seeing my progress. The painting would happen tomorrow, but the previously beat-up piece could now pass for flawless and new.

I was done, and I was tired, but I didn't move from my place on the floor. I looked from the door to the window that stared into nothingness, and an uneasy reluctance filled me.

I'd managed to make myself move from the house to the workshop without too much apprehension. Looking out over the yard from the back door before I ventured out had definitely helped my nerves. But now, I was shut inside the small building with a window that was blank and a door that opened into darkness; a darkness I couldn't survey before exposing myself to it. I knew nothing was out there, only my yard, no reason to think it unsafe, yet the fact remained:

I did not want to go out there.

I leaned my head on the wooden wall behind me, and Holly inched closer. She avoided the table without me needing to tell her and laid her head on my thigh, seeming to sense I was no longer busy and could give her attention. I ran my fingers through the thick fur along the scruff of her neck and started thinking about painting the table the next day. I was satisfied with my progress and pleased that I'd have plenty of time to do two coats and maybe even the top coat by the end of the weekend. I almost wanted to message Ivy that minute and let her know; she was usually up late anyway. But I also liked the idea of not saying anything to her until it was finished. Maybe I could come up with an excuse to have her over on Sunday night and surprise her. It was much earlier than I had told her I would have it done.

I couldn't wait to see the finished product. I had picked a sunny yellow paint that was perfect for Ivy and her eclectic decor. The table had three drawers under the surface and a bottom shelf a few inches above the floor. Two of the drawers were the right size for books, and of course she could fill the bottom shelf with books as well. The middle drawer was narrower than the other two, and I wondered what she would put in it. Bookmarks, maybe. Business cards. Her little monthly handouts the size of index cards with information about the bookshop's upcoming events: local author talks, book signings, poetry meetings, writers' workshops, open mic nights.

My thoughts drifted aimlessly, and I didn't realize I had fallen asleep until the creak of the workshop door startled me awake. I jolted from my cramped, bent position against the wall and, for a moment, couldn't understand why I was in the workshop and not in bed. Then I remembered.

And the first thing I saw was my table.

The perfect layer of white primer, smooth and clean, free of blemishes, was horribly disfigured. My eyes flew around the small space, but I was utterly alone except for Holly, who had abandoned me and moved to the far corner, curled up under the workbench. I looked back at the table. My first impression was that someone had drawn all over it, senseless scribbles and hateful diagrams etched into my work. But when I blinked the blurry sleep from my eyes, I saw that the scribbles and diagrams were on sheets of paper; Michael's papers with his drawings and notes. They had been spread across the wet surface of the table, which now looked very dry.

"No-no-no-no-no," I moaned pitifully, one hand partially covering my face so I peered at the mess through half-spread fingers, the other hand reaching toward the travesty of the table. I was terrified to touch it and see how thoroughly the papers had dried into the wood, and I was terrified to let them sit there any longer.

"What happened?" Michael's voice reverberated through the workshop. I gasped and my hand flew from the table to my heart, and I stared up at him wide-eyed.

When did he get here? I hadn't noticed him open the door, and he had not been there when I woke up.

What was that creak then? I thought a creak had woken me up, but no one had been there until now.

"I don't know what happened," I said. The moment I was tasked with speaking out loud, any poise I was clinging to disappeared and I lost control. Tears gushed from my eyes. I pulled the sleeves of my hoodie over my hands and dropped my head into them so the thick cotton could absorb the tears.

"Oh, sweetheart. What are you even doing in here?" Michael knelt beside me, leaving the door open behind him.

"I couldn't sleep and I thought I'd come out and prime the table so I could paint it tomorrow. Then when I finished, I was so tired I guess I fell asleep for a little while. And when I woke up . . . these papers were all over the table . . . " I trailed off and paused, then I had to ask it. "Did you do this?"

"Of course not." He wasn't as offended as I expected, even letting out a small, incredulous laugh. "Why would I do this?"

"I don't understand how it happened," I said, sniffing loudly. "It's not like Holly would get the papers off the counter and scatter them neatly on the table." Holly looked up and stared at me for a moment from her place in the corner before laying her head back down, unmoving.

"It had to have been a breeze," Michael said firmly. "The window is open, you know." He stroked my shoulder and kissed my head, but the thought occurred to me, a thought that almost made me shove him away in anger, though I suppressed the impulse.

"Michael," I said quietly. "A creaking noise, like the noise of a door, woke me up. But you didn't come in until after I had woken up and seen the table."

"Okay, so what are you saying?"

"If you didn't come in here before, what was that noise?"

"It was probably the back door as I was coming out!" he said, now with some irritation, but his voice dropped back into sympathy. "There is nothing funny about this, sweetheart. This isn't a cute prank. This isn't something I would ever do to you."

"I know. I'm sorry. I'm just trying to figure out what happened. Why are you even out here?"

"I woke up and you weren't there, Jana. I went looking for you and saw the workshop light on."

It made sense. I might have been used to him being missing from bed at all hours of the night, but the reverse was not the norm.

He tried to pick up the piece of paper closest to him. "Shit," he said. "It's really on there."

My face crumpled again and I dropped my head. "What a mess! What a stupid waste of time." My voice was muffled through my sleeves.

"I'm sorry," he said. "Let's go inside. It's late; we can fix it tomorrow."

I shook my head. "No, I don't want it to dry any more than it already has." I finally forced myself to touch the debacle, but my fingers met with crisp, dry paper, the pages glued firmly to the table. The extent of the damage flooded over me. "I've been asleep for hours, haven't I?" The words came out a helpless whine and, as Michael glanced at his watch and confirmed it was nearly four a.m., fresh tears welled and streamed down my face. He pulled me to my feet with determination.

"We can fix it later," he said. "After you get some sleep."

"Okay," I said, too defeated to argue, and allowed him to lead me outside.

I don't have to brave the scary, dark backyard alone now, I thought, hating myself for not closing the window and going inside immediately when I finished.

Holly followed us out and pranced through the backyard, sniffing along the perimeter of the woods, looking for a place to relieve herself, before darting to the back door to wait for us. Michael and I both paused to watch her, then he reached into the workshop and turned off the light. I turned toward the house and began walking toward Holly as Michael shut the door.

It creaked loudly as it closed.

Chapter Thirteen

I ONLY MANAGED a few hours of sleep before waking up, the thought of the table fresh in my mind. Not even bothering with coffee, I went to straight the workshop while Michael still slept. The light was pale and the grass was damp as I strode across the lawn, my face grim, my mouth set in a hard line. Holly trotted cheerfully behind me. If Michael had been up, she would have stayed by his side instead of joining me, but she wasn't allowed in the bedroom. I rolled my eyes at her when she hopped up the moment I opened the back door.

"A lot of good you did me last night," I mumbled. She gave me a dog grin, panting and wagging her tail in anticipation. She didn't seem to mind my mood or to be bothered by my attempt at guilt-tripping.

I opened the door to the workshop and stared at the table in dismay. In the back of my mind, I was hoping it was all another dream, that I would enter the workshop to find the table pristine, ready for the final, most enjoyable step: adding color. I loved starting. Around the halfway point of a painting project, I usually became worn out with it, eager to finish and sick of the color I had picked out with such early enthusiasm. But the beginning was different, with its thrill of dipping a paint brush into a new can of paint for the first time and watching the color spread, transforming an anonymous piece of furniture into my own creation. I loved it.

And now, that step would not be happening today. I stood and stared at the table. I didn't want to touch it. I looked away from the table and at the closed window, at the cheerful dawn that had transformed the yard back into a thing I knew. I hated myself for leaving the window open, hated myself for falling asleep in the workshop, and I hated that I accepted Michael's explanation without argument. It didn't make sense to me.

But what was there to say?

I sniffed, shook myself, and forced my feet to approach the table. I knelt and dragged my nails across the surface, noting the ridges of primer around the paper edges, and thought I'd be lucky if I even managed to prime it again that day. I pulled at one of the pieces of paper on the corner; it was only partially on the table, half of it flapping loosely over the edge. It looked like the easiest place to start. I pulled it up from the corner and was relieved when almost the whole piece tore away intact, though it left shreds behind like the residue of a poor-quality price sticker on a piece of plastic merchandise. I made a futile attempt at scratching the paper fragments for a moment, but they were as much a part of the table as the primer itself. I cursed and moved to the next piece.

It was much worse. From the moment I began to lift the sheet of paper, I could see it was different from the first one. This time, the piece that tore away from the table was no bigger than the width of my fingernail, the rest of the sheet holding fast to the table. I stopped and ran my hand over the piece; the primer had soaked into the paper, making it almost transparent, the writing smudged and illegible. I could still see that it was Michael's writing, his notes from his last project, and it seemed to make it all the more his fault somehow.

I began tearing along the border of the paper, but couldn't get pieces more than a centimeter long to tear off at once. I moved to the other ten or so sheets of paper and found that they were all like this one. Where the first sheet had been dropped into the paint (by the wind, supposedly) and allowed to dry, the rest were like they had been pressed into the wood—firmly, carefully, deliberately.

"Fuck!" The word spewed from my lips in a trembling shriek and Holly's head flew up from its resting place on her paws. She stared at me judgmentally for a moment before laying it down again. I sat back and dropped my head onto my knees. My entire body was trembling, and hot, angry tears welled and blurred my vision.

This looks intentional. I could not prevent the thought from surfacing, could not deny its existence, and with it came feelings so unpleasant that they took me back to a place of helpless suffering.

I had not thrived in high school. Being painfully shy, poor, having an insane mother, and not having developed the ability to laugh at myself yet were all characteristics that converged to make me an easy and frequent target. One morning, I opened my locker and was hit with the pungent, ripe smell of human urine. Someone had drenched my entire locker and everything I had in it, down to my gym clothes and the old tennis shoes I couldn't afford to replace. I had never felt so personally and insensibly hated, so deeply despised, so victimized, before that moment.

Those feelings rushed through me again as I imagined hateful fingers following my own loving ones, taking something I labored over and ruining it with all the willful malignance of an angry teenager trying to make a quiet, plain girl miserable.

I wondered if I was being tormented by a random stalker, but it seemed like too big a coincidence that it started at the same time as my dreams about Michael. Besides, I couldn't imagine that a stalker would walk into a room where I slept and leave me alone, engaging in childish vandalism instead.

And then there was Holly. Surely she wouldn't lie passive in the corner while a man she didn't know came into our space? Yet if Michael had come in, wouldn't she have rushed across the workshop to greet him, tail wagging and claws clicking against the wood floor? How would I have slept through something like that?

I couldn't understand how a breeze could have done what I was looking at, but nothing else made sense either.

I stood and stomped to the cabinets mounted along the side of the workshop and began rummaging through them, leaving a path of disarray in the carefully organized materials. I landed on the widest metal putty knife I could find, wrapped my fingers around the handle, and held it like a weapon. I attacked the table, scraping mercilessly for a few seconds without caring if I was damaging the wood in the process. I ground the metal edge against the papered surface with an aggression that made my shoulder hurt before I finally stopped and saw I was making no progress. Tiny flecks of paper gathered along the edge of the scraper, but the bulk remained firmly where it lay.

If anything, I was rubbing the paper into the wood and making it worse. It looked hopeless.

I switched to an electric sander and made better progress, sanding the surface down to fresh wood. By the time I finished, the workshop was a disaster. I was sweaty and coated in thick layers of dust, and Holly had abandoned the area entirely, escaping to a quiet patch of trees far from my noise and bad temper. I only had enough patience and energy left to clean up my mess. I put everything away, swept the workshop, and wiped down the table, then I tossed the old rags I used to the side in disgust. I doubted I could bring myself to prime it again any time soon, and gave up my dreams of a finished project that weekend.

I stepped from the workshop and stared down at my ragged tennis shoes for a moment—one of the three pairs I owned now. One for running, one for working and painting, and one for everyday use. Everyday use: a euphemism for no special use at all. Exhausted and defeated, I shook myself and moved toward the grove where I'd last seen Holly. I walked along the edge, alternating between looking at the ground as I walked and glancing up to look around for Holly. If I'd called her, she would have come instantly, but I walked along silently.

I didn't make a conscious decision to look for footprints. I didn't realize I was doing it until I reached the end of the tree line where a fence separated our yard from the neighbors', and I turned my back to the house and walked into the forest. It was a damp morning and the moisture from the soft ground chilled my feet through my shoes.

I began to feel silly. I wouldn't know when a footprint had been made even if I found one, and I likely wouldn't be able to tell if it was mine or Michael's or someone else's. I continued walking until I came across Holly lying in a patch of sunlight she'd found toward the back edge of the trees, as far from the house as she could be without digging under the barbed wire fence into the neighboring property.

"Hi, pretty girl." I knelt down and rubbed her side, enjoying the sun-soaked warmth of her fur against my chilled fingertips. "What are you doing all the way back here?"

"Jana?"

The sudden sound of Michael's voice calling from the house reached us, and Holly was on her feet in a swift, liquid motion. But she didn't move. I stayed kneeling beside her, watching.

"Holly?" the voice called.

To my shock, the call that could normally jolt her into a lightning-fast burst of movement in her eagerness to be at Michael's side had no effect. Instead, she pressed against me and rested her head on my shoulder in an unusual display of affection. She stood stock-still, her ears perked, considering.

Well, I'm not going if you're not. I stared at her, waiting to see what she would do next.

"Holly?" he called again.

Holly stared at me in silent contemplation for a moment before coming to a decision. She trotted toward the house, tracing her way deliberately through the woods. After a moment's hesitation, I followed her. When she broke through the shadows of the trees and entered the yard, we could both see Michael standing on the steps to the back porch, his eyes searching and his eyebrows knitted in confusion. His face cleared when he saw us and he said again, his voice relieved, "Holly! Come here, girl."

I watched her instead of him, and it seemed that something satisfied her in his appearance, or maybe the sight of him broke her from her lethargy. She ran to him, tail wagging, accepting his scratches and kisses with her usual excitement.

I trailed slowly behind, watching their reunion, and Michael stood and smiled when he saw me.

"What were you doing?" he asked, stepping forward to greet me. I always teased him about his willingness to kiss Holly right on the nose, and I drew back playfully when he turned from her to kiss me.

"I saw what you were doing just now," I said. I put aside my confusion about Holly's behavior, and stepped back into my usual self, our usual selves, examining Michael's mouth for signs of drool or fur.

He glanced down at Holly. "Oh, come on, there was no tongue," he said.

"Sure there wasn't," I said, but smiled and allowed him to kiss me. "We were in the grove," I said in answer to his original question. "I fixed the table. It was really bad."

"I'm so sorry, honey."

"I know. Me too."

"Can I take a look?" he asked, already walking toward the workshop. I shrugged and followed, though I dragged my feet as I walked. I didn't care to see it again. I was beginning to harbor a deep resentment for the thing that just the night before had held such interest for me, bordering on obsession, drawing me from my bed into the dark. Michael reached the workshop door before I did, and my head snapped up when he gasped, standing with the door flung wide, mouth open, eyes wide. "It's all broken!"

My stomach plummeted and I rushed to his side. I burst into the workshop to see the destruction, prepared to see nothing more than shattered splinters of wood. But as I took in the bare table and freshly swept workshop that was exactly as I left it, Michael was laughing and saying, "Just kidding! Sorry, but how crazy would that be? I was only kidding."

"That was not funny." I glared at him in angry reproach. How could he make a joke about something that obviously upset me so much?

"I'm sorry," he said, sobering instantly. "You did a great job cleaning it up. It looks like you could still finish it this weekend if you want?"

"I'm not touching it again today," I said, my voice hard. "It was a disaster, and cleaning it up was horrible. I can't stand looking at it right now." I brushed by him a little more roughly than I intended and left the workshop.

"I would have helped you fix it if you'd waited a little longer. Was it that bad?" he asked, following and closing the door behind him.

"Like I said, yes. It was really bad. The paper was completely soaked into the primer, and it couldn't be torn off at all. I had to sand the entire top layer of the table away. It was a mess."

"Wow. I had no idea it would be that bad."

"Yeah." We were standing in the yard between the workshop and the house and I gave him a hard look. "It was that bad. The paper was completely soaked in," I repeated. "It almost seemed like it was pressed into the wood."

"Shit. That's terrible." He seemed surprised. "I guess the papers must have blown onto the table while it was still soaking wet? It must have happened right after you fell asleep."

His voice lifted in a question, expecting me to agree, but I was silent.

"I guess we should've stayed and tried to clean it up last night like you wanted, so it wouldn't harden so much," he said. "I'm really sorry, honey." He stepped forward and wrapped me in a hug, not seeming to notice or care that I was covered in dust and grime and sweat, which made me feel bad about my earlier hesitation to kiss him over potential dog drool on his lips.

"I need a shower," I said.

"Okay," he said. "You go shower. I've got a pot of coffee started and I'll make us some breakfast. Sound good?"

"Thank you," I said.

We entered the house and separated at the door, me turning toward the bedroom and Michael turning toward the kitchen, Holly close on his heels. I hesitated again and turned back, watching her follow him, tracing his footsteps through the kitchen like a coordinated dance. I knew she'd eventually tire of dodging his every movement and she'd lie on the rug in front of the sink to watch him. I knew it because it was what she always did. Exhausted and depressed, I tried to push away the unease that lingered and turned away from their dance to take my shower.

Chapter Fourteen

WHY IS HE *whispering?*

I hung suspended between sleep and wakefulness one night, and I didn't know if my dreaming self was the one wondering it, didn't know where the question came from, only knew that it existed, tugging at my mind.

So many nights, sweet nothings murmured in my ear. I'd wonder what he was trying to accomplish; if he wanted to wake me up, he could shake me awake and talk to me.

It continued like that. Sometimes I would be in the middle of a dream about something else, at work or talking to Ivy or back in my childhood home, and his voice would begin playing in the background, a low murmur that steadily rose until it began distracting me from working or talking or remembering, until eventually I left the dream, left my sleep, and opened my eyes to see nothing but an empty room.

Other nights, I was woken up by the sound of him coming into our room and he would sit down on the bed next to me and by the next morning I only had vague memories of him talking to me as I drifted to sleep, remembering only snatches of what he said.

Hi, beautiful.

Were you having a good dream?

Are you tired?

Get some sleep, then.

I love you.

I wanted to know if it was real, but after our fight I didn't dare to ask him directly.

Until one night changed my mind. I was curled on my side facing the doorway sleeping. Or maybe I was only trying to fall asleep. It was hard to know.

The rattle of the doorknob, a narrow strip of light, a shape passing through the doorway, the light extinguished. His weight on the edge of the bed in front of me.

"Did I wake you?" he asked.

"No, I don't think so."

His hand moving under the covers to squeeze my side.

"I feel like I didn't get to see you much today."

"We were a little busy, huh?"

His hand traced my arm from my wrist where it curled in front of my chest, then up to my shoulder. "You've been working some long hours lately."

"End of the fiscal year for a lot of our clients," I said. "It's a busy time. It will be over soon."

"Imagine how busy we'll be when we have kids."

I blinked. Tried to see him more clearly in the darkness. I couldn't remember the last time we had talked about kids.

"When?" I asked.

Not if? I thought of all the times we had talked about it, and we had always ended up saying neither of us were sure what we wanted; that we were open to it, but not set on it. It was my only justification for not telling him. We said we could be happy either way.

"Why not?" he asked. "Imagine seeing a little you and a little me all wrapped up in one little human."

"That would be something."

He planted an arm behind me and swung his leg onto the bed, holding himself suspended above me, his weight lightly pressing against me. He lowered his head and kissed my neck as I lay pinned between his arms. Then he shifted and dropped on his side behind me. His body filled the spaces behind me like a liquid, his knees pressed against the back of mine, his arm running across my stomach beneath my arm, his face in my hair. I fell back asleep in his arms.

***

The next day, I stared at him pensively over my mug during our coffee time. It was a quiet weekend morning and we were lying on the cushioned wicker couch on our back porch. I kept finding myself studying him when he wasn't looking, tracing the familiar line of his profile. Wondering.

It was winter, but it was one of those unseasonably warm Missouri days that could happen with little warning in the middle of December, indistinguishable from a cheerful spring morning.

The sun was bright and streamed directly into our little pocket of the house reserved for peace. I was wearing the faded cotton shorts I'd slept in, along with long, fuzzy socks and an oversized sweater I'd pulled on over my tank top before stepping out the back door. Michael wore a white t-shirt and dark blue pajama pants, and my bare legs were draped over his lap. He held his coffee in the hand furthest from me, and the fingertips of his other hand dragged along my leg, lazily tracing my shin bone from my ankle to my knee and back again.

I can grow old like this. Do you want that, too? I asked him silently. *What* do *you want?*

He faced the backyard and sat in peaceful silence as my eyes traveled over his face. The relaxed corner of his mouth, the way his nose tilted up ever so slightly at the tip, the light stubble on his cheeks and neck. Every feature was familiar. I knew how his face would feel against my lips if I leaned forward to kiss it. I could smell his scent before it reached my nostrils, see the glow of his smile when he would turn to kiss me back.

Do you whisper in my ear while I sleep? I imagined asking him, smiling softly to myself with derision. I would sound ludicrous. Again.

Have you been talking to me at night?

No. Still accusatory. Still enough to make me sound confused. Disjointed.

Did you ruin my table? Do you want me to think I'm crazy?

My eyes watered at the last thought and I pushed it away. He couldn't be that cruel.

This is Michael, you silly child. You could just tell him.

"I've had dreams lately about you talking to me when you come to bed." The words rang in my ears when they were said out loud, too loud in the still, silent morning, reverberating through our little pocket of peace.

He looked at me, a slight cloud over his previously open, clear expression. "Saying what?"

You tricked him, you know, you know you did. Laughing and cheerful and carefree on all those dates. You certainly didn't seem like a mess, did you? But these things run in the family.

"Mostly telling me goodnight, you love me, sleep well, that kind of thing," I said, my tone light and casual. "I don't remember much else." *That you want me to have your child.*

"Mm. Better than your other dreams," he said with a smile, and I relaxed. "I never talk to you while you're sleeping, though."

"I know," I assured him quickly. But then I had to ask. "What about last night? Did we talk in bed before we went to sleep?"

"No. You were sound asleep when I came in."

"Okay." I gave him a sunny smile. "Just a dream, then."

I was proud of myself for navigating the issue so skillfully, even while my heart sank because it wasn't the answer I wanted.

Of course. I just like to tell you goodnight. I didn't think it bothered you. If only that had been his answer. How easy that would have made everything. And somehow, illogically, I was hurt. Even though I panicked at the idea that he had decided that kids were an absolute in our future, I was hurt that it had only been the Michael in my mind who wanted to discuss it, and not the Michael before me.

And I wasn't satisfied with his answer. It was too hard for me to believe it was all in my head.

And the dreams continued while I continued avoiding talking to Michael about them directly. Through innocuous questions with veiled intent, I confirmed which of my interactions, conversations, and vague memories were him and which were not. I didn't want to fight again, didn't want him to give me that look again, that look of betrayal and disbelief like he couldn't believe something so absurd was coming from someone he loved.

But it was impossible not to make a mistake eventually.

Chapter Fifteen

I **WAS LYING** on the couch reading one evening when I drifted into a light sleep. I didn't know I was cold until the sudden pressure of a blanket being laid over me sent a pleasant warmth through me, and I burrowed more deeply into the couch as Michael knelt to speak in a low voice at my side, his light, warm breath brushing my cheek.

"Are you comfortable?" he asked.

I nodded and moaned softly, not opening my eyes, not wanting to wake up. He was in the habit of waking me up whenever I fell asleep on the couch, urging me to go to bed so I would sleep through the night and wouldn't wake up with a sore back or neck. It was thoughtful of him, but I didn't want to get up and go to bed. I didn't want to move or speak.

"Do you want to stay here?" he asked.

"Mmm," I nodded again.

"Okay," he said. "I'll let you sleep here for a little while." His lips touched my forehead and he turned off the lights that were piercing through my closed eyelids, allowing me to relax them in relief. I plunged into a deep sleep.

I woke up several hours later, after midnight, in stark darkness, covered in a light sweat. I had the rush of disorientation that follows an impromptu nap. I was guilty and confused, my body stiff and worn. I blinked in the darkness, the house's stillness pressing heavily on my chest. Pushing the blanket away, I rose quickly and switched on the light. I turned from the empty room and forced myself not to run up the stairs in my desperation to see another face, to banish the nervous dread I'd woken up with, and I wandered into the soft, welcoming light of Michael's office, reassured to see him at his computer. Holly rested at his feet. He looked up and smiled at me.

"Hi, beautiful."

"Hi," I said as I approached him. "You're right. I shouldn't sleep on the couch."

"I am usually right," he answered.

I leaned against him and he wrapped one arm around my legs, resting his chin on my hip and staring up at me from his desk chair. I ran my fingers through his hair and continued, "I feel awful now. I'm stiff and sore and I feel like I need a shower. I'm sure I'll have a hard time getting back to sleep for the rest of the night."

"I'm sorry, sweetie. Why were you sleeping on the couch?"

"Well, it's your fault," I said. "You made me all cozy."

"How did I make you cozy?"

I immediately sensed my error and my secure peacefulness froze into cold discomfort. I looked around the room with a shiver.

"Oh, another dream I guess." I tried to say it without concern. "I was napping downstairs and I thought you came and covered me with a blanket."

"Nope. I've been buried in work and lost track of time. I thought you were reading out there. I didn't even realize you fell asleep."

I shrugged, feigning nonchalance. "I was tired."

"At least you're dreaming of me doing nice things now, instead of all the creepy cuddling."

"Yes," I smiled. Better to make it a joke. "Creepy Michael has improved. You're almost decent."

"Damn right," he said, rising and stretching before wrapping me in his arms. "I think I'm actually ready for bed too."

He turned off his computer screen, and we walked together from the room. Holly rose and stretched when he did, then she darted in front of us, heading for her bed.

I was relieved to keep him next to me. It occurred to me as we walked slowly down the stairs, shoulders bumping back and forth down the narrow steps, fingers intertwined, that my dreams had changed. That ever since our fight, none of my dreams had been threatening, violent, or physical at all. I had welcomed the change with relief.

But now, in the back of my mind, I began to wonder if I was only being tricked more effectively.

After we reached our bedroom and changed for bed and brushed our teeth, I was hit with a realization I'd been puzzling over in the back of my mind since I woke. The blanket. Michael climbed into bed and looked at me, waiting for me to join him. I stayed rooted where I was, standing next to my side of the bed.

"Are you coming?" he asked.

"Michael." I looked directly at him and said it so sharply he jumped a little. "What if something's really happening? The table, and now this. We've been thinking they're dreams and not seriously thinking someone could be coming in here, into our home, but when I woke up, there was a blanket covering me. An actual blanket was on top of me when I woke up."

He looked at me blankly.

"I did not cover myself with a blanket," I pressed on. "And those papers on the table, they didn't seem like they just fell there. It was like someone pressed them into the wood. And there was that time on your birthday, I thought I saw you, but it had to have been someone else. What if he was following us? And once, I saw someone walk through our front yard early in the morning before you were awake. What if someone is doing this to me?" The words tumbled out so quickly I could barely keep up with my own thoughts, and by the time I finished, I could feel the heat in my flushed face.

Michael stared at me, worried, and ran a hand through his hair, pausing to rub his scalp for a moment.

"I don't know, hon. I would've thought it was something like that from the beginning, except that you said it was me you were seeing. You think you have a stalker who looks just like me?"

It was the same argument I had had with myself when I considered the possibility the first time. But I was scared now. I had never seriously worried that any of the things I had experienced inside our home were the result of someone breaking in, and it didn't make sense to me now. It was Michael. Dreams or reality, it was Michael.

At least, I thought it was.

But when I thought of the blanket and even the slightest possibility that someone else was doing these things to me, it didn't matter what the truth was. I wanted him to start taking this seriously.

It took swallowing every ounce of pride I had to answer, "Maybe I was wrong about that."

If there was someone coming into our home, we needed to do

something about it, whether it all made sense or not. No matter who it looked like.

"Okay," he said. He threw the covers aside and stood. "Is the back door locked?"

"Yes," I said. "We can double check, but it should be locked since I was the last one through it." I strode from the room and he followed me, ignoring the soft jab. He had grown up in an area where it was normal to leave doors unlocked at night and I had not, and it showed. Michael was terrible about leaving windows unshut and doors ajar, and I'd had to personally break him of the habit of leaving his keys in his unlocked car.

When we got to the back door together, I wiggled the knob, demonstrating that it was shut and locked securely. Our eyes met and we walked to the front door next. Michael checked that one, and this time his eyes met mine in worried guilt.

"It's not locked," he said.

I found myself twisting the hair at the back of my skull again as I stared at the door.

"I got the mail earlier," he confessed. "I guess I forgot."

Could someone really have stepped right through our door, knelt beside me while I slept, whispered in my ear . . .

The violation took the air from my chest. Michael saw the fear in my eyes and covered the short distance between us in a quick step, wrapping me in a hug. I was surprised to feel him shaking and hear his heart pounding, fast and hard. For a moment I thought he was afraid, but I glanced up at the bright red splotches on his cheeks and saw that his mouth was set in a hard line, and his jaw twitched under the force with which he clenched it.

He was angry.

I stepped back and looked at him. "What are you thinking?" I asked.

"I'm thinking that I can't believe we've been arguing about dreams when someone might have been walking into our house and hurting you, and planning God knows what else." His voice shook in rage, and Holly left her corner of the living room where she slept to stand next to him, staring up at him in concern.

"I don't know anything for sure," I said. "I think some of it was dreams. The nights with you in bed, I can't wrap my mind around that being someone else." I shuddered. "It was you. Dreams of you."

"Didn't you say it could've been someone else and you only thought it was me?"

"For some of it, maybe. Like tonight, with the blanket."

Are you comfortable? The voice played in my mind again and I felt his breath on my cheek, and I wondered if it was really possible that it wasn't Michael.

"And the man in the doorway," I continued. "And the table; I didn't see anyone when the table happened."

"You keep bringing up the table. What do you think happened?"

"I told you, it was like someone pressed the paper into the primer."

"You think someone snuck into the workshop, put paper all over the table, and snuck back out?"

"Yes," I said, my voice breaking a little. It sounded ridiculous.

"And Holly?" He sounded almost argumentative now. "She was in the workshop with you. It's hard enough to believe someone could just walk into our living room, even with her being upstairs with me. She's upstairs with me all day during the week and she still jumps to attention and starts barking if someone even comes close to our front door. Even if this guy was somehow quiet enough that she didn't hear it happen tonight, I can't imagine that she would've just sat there in the workshop and watched a stranger walk around while you slept."

"I don't know! Maybe he found a way to make friends with her."

"I'm calling the police," he said.

"And telling them what?" I was flustered and confused at Michael's questioning, even when I knew he only wanted to help. I couldn't imagine how questioning with police officers would go. "The only tangible thing we have is the blanket. You barely believe me about the table, and everything else might or might not be dreams." I was dismayed when tears began to well as I spoke. "Even the blanket thing probably sounds questionable to someone with doubts about any of it. Doubts about me. I'll just sound crazy." At the last word, whatever barrier was keeping the tears in check broke and they spilled out over my cheeks.

It wasn't like Michael to look uncertain, but he looked uncertain now, his stare moving from my face to the door, then darting around our home apprehensively, and back to my face.

"Okay," he said, finally. "We won't call the police. Yet. But maybe we should be on our guard for a while now. We can get a security system; it's something we've been talking about anyway."

"Okay," I said, wrapping my arms around myself to keep from fidgeting.

"I want you to pay attention to your surroundings at work, during your commute, wherever you go, okay?" he continued. "We need to figure out if someone's following you around. We'll put some motion lights outside so they light up if anyone walks by. Maybe security cameras on the entrances."

Relief washed over me as he spoke. I felt like an idiot for not having asked for this right away. For being so insecure about sounding paranoid, so terrified of being seen as delusional or unstable, that I was willing to ignore signs of a dangerous stalker. Or being too busy suspecting Michael to think someone else was the cause.

Yet . . . his hands, his lips, his voice . . .

But it didn't matter that it didn't make sense. It didn't matter which parts were in my head, which parts were dreams, which parts might be a dangerous stalker, or whether there was a stalker at all. I was scared, scared like I hadn't been since I was a small child listening to strange noises in the night that I didn't have an explanation for yet, and I wanted something to be done. I wanted to walk outside without wondering what might be out there. I wanted to stop being afraid of dark corners in my own home.

"Okay," I said, and hesitated. "Should we . . . get a weapon?" I was reluctant to suggest a gun, not sure if it would sound like an overreaction. He stared at me again, thinking. Maybe he didn't trust me with a gun.

"You take pepper spray on your runs already, right?" he asked, and I nodded. "Okay. Start keeping that with you all the time for a while, okay?" I nodded again.

Why am I letting him decide? I can get a gun if I want to. But I knew nothing about guns, while he had grown up with them. I didn't even know where to start with getting a license, or what kind of license I'd need, or what would be required to get one.

"I'll look into the security system, lights, and all that tomorrow while you're at work," he said. "And maybe we can get a stun gun." He still didn't suggest a real gun. Maybe he didn't believe there was anything to fear; maybe the security measures were only to placate me. A gun might be a reasonable response to being stalked or having your home broken into, but not so reasonable simply to calm your overly imaginative wife. I wasn't sure which was his motivation.

"Okay," I said, swallowing everything else.

My mind took stock of the possibilities again. Dreams, stalker, Michael, crazy. At that point, I could have believed a little of everything.

Chapter Sixteen

WHEN THE SECURITY cameras were installed, everything stopped for a while. By the second week of no dreams, no odd events, no strange conversations, I was in the mood to celebrate. Shortly after dinner, Michael settled on the couch to watch television and I paced through the living room, trying to decide what to do with myself. I was happily restless, almost giddy with satisfaction over how well the upgraded security had worked.

Maybe it was all in my head. All I needed was some peace of mind.

I noticed Michael watching me with an amused smile. "What are you up to, honey?" he asked.

"I'm not sure," I said, returning his smile with one twice as large. "Maybe I'll go work out. Or read. Or bake something. Do you feel like something sweet?" I was feeling indulgent.

"If you want to make something, I'm sure I'll eat it," he answered, noncommittal. It was already dark out, and I needed him to be more enthusiastic if I was going to be daring enough to bake cookies at night, so I dismissed that idea.

"Ooh, maybe I'll take a bath. Light some candles and read. I might take a glass of wine, too."

"Ooh!" He mirrored the sound I made. "What's the occasion?"

"Nothing. I just feel like relaxing." I leaned over him and kissed him, then headed for the bedroom. I hadn't had a bath in ages.

Preparing the bath was like performing an old ritual; refamiliarizing myself with the customs, muscle memory taking me through the motions. While the tub filled with steaming water, I made sure I had everything I needed. I hung my fluffy bathrobe on the door and carefully placed a soft, fresh towel on a stool within arm's reach of the tub. I poured salts into the water and inhaled the floral scents as they dissolved, then turned to the candles. I turned off the overhead lights so the bathroom was illuminated only by the soft, flickering glow from the flames. I chose an old paperback from my nightstand, one I wouldn't mind getting a little damp, and positioned it on the side of the tub where it would be easy to reach if I wanted it.

When the tub was filled about three-quarters I stepped in, a thrill of pleasure and slight pain running through me as I lowered myself into the hot water. I allowed myself to relax completely for what felt like the first time in weeks, watched the flames dance against the wall through half-closed eyes, and let my mind wander.

Was it all in my head? It was hard to imagine a real-life threat, a stranger so brazen as to come into our home while I slept, with Michael awake in the next room, being so easily solved, dissuaded by security cameras, our very first countermove. But maybe it was enough.

I kept getting stuck on the blanket. I pictured it in my mind, thick blue knit, folded over the edge of the couch next to my feet. I knew I fell asleep without it. It wasn't within arm's reach; I would have had to sit up and stretch, stretching down to my toes to grab it, unfold it, and spread it over myself. It was heavy and tightly folded; I couldn't imagine doing all of that in my sleep.

But there were so many things I'd done without realizing it. Just that morning, I had gotten to work a little early because I knew I needed to print off several documents before an eight a.m. meeting. When I arrived, they were already there in a neat stack on my desk, ready for the meeting. When I saw them, I remembered vaguely thinking of the documents the day before and reminding myself that I needed them; it wasn't a stretch to realize I must have gone a step further and printed them before I left work, saving myself from rushing in the morning and risking going to the meeting unprepared.

And then there was him. As soon as he drifted into my mind, his whispers—*are you comfortable*—and his lips against my forehead, and perhaps more than anything, his thoughtfulness; his understanding that I was too comfortable to move, that the only things keeping me from being completely and perfectly satisfied were the cold air against my bare arms and legs and the light against my eyelids.

Yet if I dreamed him, of course he would know those things.

"You look comfortable." Michael's voice from the doorway

brought me back to the present and I jumped, splashing water over the candles nearest to me. He laughed. "Sorry, honey. I thought you heard me come in."

I took a deep breath and tried not to look too irritated as I met his eyes. He gave me a rueful smile and grabbed the lighter from the sink, then knelt by the tub to relight the candles that were extinguished in the splash. He rested his chin on my damp arm that was draped over the edge of the tub.

"Am I interrupting?" he asked. "I can go."

"No, it's fine," I said. "What are you up to?"

"Just checking on you." He wrapped his fingers around my hand and gave it a small squeeze, then began dragging his fingertips along my arm, tracing my skin slowly up to my elbow, then to my shoulder, then up my neck and along my ear. I closed my eyes and rested my head on the back of the tub as he moved his hand into my hair and began to massage my scalp.

"Do you want me to wash your hair?" he asked.

"That sounds nice," I said, without opening my eyes. He shifted and reached across me for the shampoo. He turned the water back on and held a cup beneath the flow—I hadn't realized he'd brought one with him until I heard the water filling it—and turned the water back off when the cup was full. He nudged my back gently to tell me I should lean forward. I complied, and he held one hand across the top of my forehead and used the other to pour hot water over my head. Then he filled his palm with shampoo, rubbed it on his hands, and began to lather it through my hair.

I had never had anyone wash my hair for me before Michael, except when I got it cut. It never sounded appealing to me. The first time he offered, I accepted because I didn't want to sound ungrateful, but I expected to suffer through having my hair pulled, the wrong water temperature used, and my scalp either scraped painfully or missed entirely. I was surprised at how wrong I was; Michael was intuitive in knowing exactly how much pressure to use, gentle in working through tangles, and left me feeling thoroughly clean and relaxed.

He turned the water back on and began rinsing out the shampoo, putting conditioner on his hands so he could work his fingers through without getting caught in the tangles. He didn't speak. Every now and then, he leaned over and kissed my shoulder or let his hand fall down my back, rubbing the muscles under my shoulder blades and along my spine until his hand dipped below the water, then he ran his fingers back up and through my hair again.

When he was finished, he motioned for me to lay my head back down, then he rested his chin on the side of the tub again and stared at me with a small smile. "How do you feel?" he asked.

"That was lovely. Thank you." My voice was a low, lazy murmur.

His smile grew. "Well, I'll let you finish your bath. I'm tempted to join."

"That sounds nice," I said, unsure if I meant it.

"I won't disturb you anymore, though. Enjoy, sweetheart." He pushed himself to his feet. He walked toward the door, paused with his hand on the doorknob, and half-turned to look at me again, the dim candlelight casting a strange glow across his face. "Be careful not to fall asleep in there, now," he said.

"I won't," I promised.

Feeling a sense of peace with myself, Michael, and our lives that I hadn't felt in weeks, I closed my eyes and worked on making my mind blank. To let go of the dreams and the fighting. To stop thinking about the table or the blanket. To forget about the security system and why we got it.

I stayed where I was until the water lost its warmth. By the time I pulled myself up, my legs were wobbly and my hair was partially dry. I wrapped myself in my robe and drained the water, stretching and yawning. I was ready for bed. I wandered barefoot through the bedroom to find Michael and say goodnight. I went down the hall to find him in the living room watching television, Holly curled up beside him, his fingers tucked into her thick black fur. He paused the television when I came in.

"I just came to say goodnight," I said as I approached.

"Already? Did your bath tire you out?"

As though on cue, I stifled a loud yawn as I answered, "Actually, yes."

"Okay." He rose and gave me a kiss. "Good night, sweetheart." He sat back down and scratched Holly's head.

"Good night. Thank you for washing my hair," I said.

"What are you talking about?" He glanced up at me, his face a blank. "I didn't wash your hair."

I froze where I was standing and the color drained from my

face, while he continued rubbing Holly's ears and began softly praising her for being a very good, smart, and beautiful girl.

I reeled. *I saw him,* I thought. I saw his face; the light was dim, but I saw his face, stared into his eyes. I was not asleep.

My hand went to my hair; it was wet and clean and smelled of my shampoo. I did not wash it myself.

Oh god oh god I might puke...

He glanced up and his expression changed when he saw my face. "Jana," he said, filled with concern. "You can't think I'm serious."

I blinked at him without comprehension for a moment, then the change of emotions from fear to anger came so quickly it made me dizzy. "What?"

"I was joking. That was obviously a joke," he said, and I bristled at the condescension in his voice.

"Do you really think that was an okay joke to make?" My voice was trembling, and I hated to hear it.

"Did you really think that wasn't me? You looked right at me, sweetie." He turned off the television and leaned forward, his knees spread apart, his hands folded between them. He gazed at me steadily, questions in his eyes. "I was just trying to make a joke because of all the weird dreams. Since everything's been fine, I thought . . . We talked. Face to face. How could you think that didn't happen? Did you believe for a moment that could be someone else?" So many questions in his eyes.

What else do you believe?

If you don't know your own husband, what do you know?

How can I trust you with anything?

"No, of course not," I said. "I thought for a second I had fallen asleep and had a nightmare."

"Are your dreams that realistic?" he asked, so much doubt in his voice. "We talked, I washed your hair . . . I was in there for a good half hour, honey."

"Yeah, I know," I answered, becoming defensive. "If I had had a second to think about it, I would have realized you were kidding, of course. I just got scared for a second. It wasn't a funny joke to make."

"You're right," he said. "I shouldn't have. I didn't think you would take me seriously."

I bit my tongue and refused to defend myself any further. He was the one being thoughtless.

"I'm going to bed," I said abruptly, closing the conversation.

"Oh, come on," he said, rising quickly and moving to block me from the hallway. "I said I'm sorry."

"Did you, though? Or did you just make me feel bad for falling for a joke you shouldn't have made?"

"What do you mean? How did I make you feel bad?"

"Do I really need to spell this out for you?" I started to wonder if he enjoyed putting me on the spot, dragging all my insecurities out for him to poke at them. "You're acting like it's ridiculous that I would get worried for a moment, with everything that's happened."

"I mean, I know I shouldn't have made the joke, and I am sorry. But even if there was someone doing any of this, a stalker or whatever, there couldn't have been any question about it being me who was washing your hair. It's not like I put on a mask and started peeping in windows to mess with you or anything like that."

His tone about a stalker was dismissive; the time that had passed without incident had distanced him from his initial fear and concern, had made it far-fetched again. Had brought him back to blaming me, explaining everything as figments of my imagination. Irritation bubbled in my chest at his thoughtlessness, his lack of concern. It was the kind of irritation that had no rationality, no understanding, no affection, and I knew I needed to get away from him.

"We're talking in circles now," I said, doing my best to keep the anger from my voice so he would allow the issue to lie. "Let's forget about it. It's fine." I reluctantly allowed him to wrap me in a hug and kiss me goodnight, putting a convincing smile on my face in hopes that it would be enough to end the conversation.

"I really am sorry," he said, kissing my head. "I didn't mean to freak you out."

What possible purpose could that joke have but to freak me out?

"I know. Don't worry about it. Goodnight."

"I love you," he said.

"Love you too."

I left him with relief to go to bed alone.

I lay on my back in the dark, hands folded across my stomach, staring at the blank void that was our ceiling, still smoldering. Had he ever believed in the possibility of a real danger? His anger and concern had certainly seemed real. Yet here he was, back to making jokes.

Maybe it was his way of expressing relief, I reasoned, defending him to myself. Maybe he was also feeling more relaxed tonight, looser, after so many days of peace.

Yet the way he let his words linger. My shoulders stiffened in discomfort and my fingers curled against my palms at the thought, picturing him sitting there, not looking at me while I panicked, focused on Holly.

I knew before it happened that it would. That he would follow me into the bedroom, unable to let the matter rest. The door breathed a sliver of light into the room that disappeared behind his shadow, and then he was sitting beside me on the bed, like so many other nights.

"You're still upset, aren't you?"

"A little," I admitted.

"I didn't mean to upset you." He found my hands where they were resting on my stomach and intertwined his fingers with mine.

"I believe you," I said.

"But you're still upset." He let out a soft sigh.

"It doesn't feel good to have your fears laughed at." I felt whiny and punitive the moment the words escaped my lips. He had already apologized.

"I know. Your fears are not something to laugh at."

That wasn't reassuring. "It's okay," I said. "Let's forget about it."

"Thank you." He climbed into bed behind me and wrapped me in a cold embrace, his body temperature a shock against my own, warm under the covers. And we stayed like that, until he fell asleep after a while. I stayed awake for a long time.

CHAPTER SEVENTEEN

A COUPLE DAYS after our argument, I had a presentation. I didn't mind giving presentations as much as most people did. As much as you'd probably expect someone like me to. I'd treat them like a play; rehearse like I would for a leading role; and put on my Professional, Knowledgeable Jana costume before I went on.

"Marketing needs to understand our services better if we expect them to sell those services for us," Devin told me a few weeks before, when he asked me to do it. "You're so good at explaining complicated topics so that anyone can understand them." Always the compliment, because it wouldn't sound nearly as good to say you want someone to do something because you don't feel like it. "Do you think you could handle it?"

"Of course," I answered. "I'd be happy to."

I had learned in my first month that my coworkers throughout the firm never asked anyone to give presentations, never called them by that name. It was always 'sitting down with' or 'giving a quick overview' or 'providing education'. 'Presenting' was strictly taboo.

That day, I had prepared to tell one of my favorites: the small-town granny. Evelyn Baker worked at First Community Bank, Lillyville; a town with a population of a couple thousand, the kind of town with one main street that had a few restaurants, a gas station, more banks than it seemed to need, and not much else.

I introduced myself to the room of people who looked vaguely familiar from crossing paths in the break room, hallways, and bathrooms, then gave an overview of my team's services. The only person in the room I knew by name was Maria, who Devin had suggested sit in. Maybe so that one day I could tell her she was really good at explaining things.

"I can give an example of one of the first accounts I worked on, if anyone's interested?" I asked after my introduction. The group nodded their assent, and I launched into the story.

Evelyn Baker had worked at the bank for more than forty years and had never missed a day. She sat at a desk right next to the front entrance, and she greeted each and every customer that came in, most of them by name. She had bright plastic chairs for children next to her desk, one red and one blue to match the bank's own patriotic colors, with a coloring station equipped not only with crayons but also with glue sticks, googly eyes, and stickers that she supplied herself. The bank clients happily deposited their children to wait with Evelyn while they took care of business. Children or not, almost everyone paused at her desk for a moment to chat and exchange pleasantries before continuing on to the tellers' counter. And if any customers needed help setting up or adding money to an investment fund, they paused at her desk longer, because Evelyn would help with that.

There was a little something extra about Evelyn. She didn't only remember her clients' names and their children's names and ask about their families, injuries, illnesses, recent sporting events, and anything else they might have had going on in their lives. It wasn't that she made every bank customer feel special. It wasn't that she was such a reliable feature of the bank that arriving there and seeing no Evelyn would be like the front door was missing, either. All of those things were true, but what was perhaps most important was that she was genuinely good at her job and she went above and beyond for each and every client.

At other banks, customers sat down with a senior employee like Evelyn and they talked about their investment options, filled out their paperwork, and provided their personal information. And then they took their checks or their cash and they walked to the teller window to deposit their first investment into their newly opened account.

That was not how it worked at First Community Bank, Lillyville.

At First Community Bank, Lillyville, once the investment options were explored and the paperwork was completed and the personal information was provided, Evelyn smiled at her clients and said, "I'll get this all taken care of for you." She let them sit comfortably in their cushioned chairs in front of her desk, often with their children happily situated in the plastic ones, while she took their initial deposits to the teller window for them.

Above and beyond.

And somewhere on that brief trip from Evelyn's desk at the front door to the teller window, something happened.

$1,500 became $1,400.

$5,000 became $4,500.

$9,400 became an even $8,000.

She edited writing on checks, she discreetly pulled bills from envelopes full of cash, she had clients sign their checking withdrawal and investment account deposit slips and then she added the numbers in afterward.

I was in the groove as I told the familiar story to faces more interested than when I'd started, but it was around this point in the story that heat began to rise in my face and my voice faltered slightly. I wasn't sure why; I hadn't gotten so nervous during a presentation since high school.

What's my problem today? I cleared my throat and took a sip of water to cover.

Where was I? I tried to remember if I had already explained how Evelyn did it and how she did it so well, but I was blanking.

I never understood this one. I shouldn't have picked this story.

"How did they catch her?" The question brought me back to the group and I wondered how long I had paused; had I trailed off? I knew I had begun the presentation as planned, I had given an overview of my department, and then I began going through the Evelyn Baker case study, but now I was dizzy and confused.

"I'm sorry?" I asked, trying to buy time to regain my bearings.

I'd told that story dozens of times; why was my chest tight? Was my face as red as it felt? Could they tell my hands were trembling from across the room?

"How did they catch her?" Random Young Marketing Guy repeated his question patiently.

"Um, she confessed," I said. "The bank was getting an audit, as they did every year, and this time they called in my team because they knew something was off but they didn't know what. They probably would have eventually found her out even without our help; she was constantly robbing Peter to pay Paul, as they say; she was pulling from one account to satisfy withdrawals from another."

Did I really just use that expression? And did my accent just slip back into my voice?

"She was keeping track of everything by hand," I continued, forcing my words to be clear and calm. "She was writing it down in a small notebook she kept right there in her desk. Anyone could have opened her drawer and seen it there. But no one thought to."

Breathe. In, out. I clenched my hands under the table in my efforts to control them.

"It sounds like your team didn't actually do anything to catch her?"

"Well, it wasn't a very sophisticated scam. I do honestly think we would have found the issue within hours. And I think she knew that. Which is why she walked into the offices we were using within a few minutes of us arriving, and she told us everything."

Oh, Evelyn, so tired of hiding. I almost thought I might cry.

What is wrong with me? I have to get out of here.

"So, as you can imagine, one of our biggest challenges is that either we find something, which makes the client very unhappy because someone's been stealing from them, or we don't find anything, which makes the client question the value of our services . . . "

Okay, good, I can do this.

I finished my speech as quickly as I could, distracted by how panicked Evelyn's story made me. Most scammers like Evelyn don't get away with it because they're good at it, or because they have everyone fooled so well, or because they've thought of answers to any questions. They get away with it because no one wants to ask the questions in the first place, and because no one wants to think they can be fooled.

It's the same mentality that makes people think only other people's spouses cheat on them, I realized. *We all like to think we're special. We like to think we know better.*

I slipped from the room the moment I finished, without asking if anyone had more questions, avoiding meeting Maria's eyes. I fled to my office and closed the door, then collapsed with relief into my chair. My eyes landed on the picture of me and Michael on our wedding day. I thought of his joke the night before. What if he had taken it further, continued to deny washing my hair?

I would have blamed myself. I would have had no choice but to think it was a dream, or that I was going insane, or maybe I would have gone a step further and started thinking I was being haunted.

Haunted by my own husband?

What made me better than an entire town who saw only a harmless grandmother, a professional bank employee, a helpful, kind woman when they looked at Evelyn Baker? Than her spouse, children, and grandchildren who never would have dreamed to question that her generosity and lavish Christmas gifts could be explained by anything but careful money management and frugality? What made me immune to being fooled as thoroughly as they were?

Nothing.

Chapter Eighteen

"**A**NOTHER MARTINI?" Michael asked with a smile as he walked into the kitchen that evening. There was no judgment in his voice; he asked it as simply as he would ask if I was about to take a shower or watch television. Yet still his appearance startled me, as though I had been caught in the act of something shameful. But Michael didn't think of drinking the same way I did. I remembered the first holiday I spent with his family, being shocked at the amount of alcohol out in the open, readily available instead of hidden in closets and drawers like my childhood self had assumed it belonged. I was even more shocked when no one drank too much of it.

I paused and stared for a moment at the gin in my hands. It was the third night in a row that I had held the now almost-empty bottle.

I wondered if Michael realized it too; if he had been paying attention.

I continued to pour. At least I hadn't had any dreams lately, and maybe it was because of the security system, or maybe it was because a drink before bed helped me sleep. *Besides, I am an adult*, I reasoned. I could have a drink after a long day if I wanted.

And it's Friday. Just a nightcap, as they used to say...

"Yes. Long day," I said. "Do you want one?"

He considered, staring with uncertain interest at the drink in my hand. Hungry for something, but what?

"Nah, I think I'm good tonight," he said, crossing instead to the fridge. "Why was your day long?"

"Presentation," I answered, offering no further explanation. He wasn't paying attention anyway. He opened the fridge and I watched with amusement as he stared with even more uncertain interest at the drawer filled with assorted fruit—oranges, apples, and berries—while his eyes darted to the freezer.

We all know you want to reach for the ice cream. Just do it. Who are you trying so hard for?

My eyes followed him through every careless movement and thought that flitted openly across his face. All the ease and comfort of someone who had no reason to think they would have anything other than a restful, peaceful night's sleep in a few hours.

I had to wonder if the man who made jokes to make me feel crazy, who laughed about the horrible thing that happened to my table, the same man who as a teenager had the patience to sneak out to a cold barn in the blackest morning hours and lie in wait, freezing and alone, and all for a good laugh . . . I had to wonder if a man like that would find it funny to lie to me about the things he did, making me think they were dreams.

Would a man like that stop the prank when the cameras went up?

I glanced down to see that I had already finished half my drink before Michael had a chance to decide between a healthy snack versus joining me in his own version of indulgence, and I set the drink decisively on the counter. I needed to slow down.

I hoped he hadn't noticed how quickly I was drinking it. I tried to reassure myself that maybe he hadn't seen how full it was to begin with. Michael finally closed the fridge and turned around with a smile. He held an apple in his hand, successfully avoiding temptation and wearing his childish triumph unselfconsciously on his face.

"What are you going to do tonight?" he asked.

"I'm about to read for a little while before I head to bed," I said. "What about you?"

"I was thinking of going out to the workshop," he said. His current project was a chair, started almost immediately after I finished Ivy's table, even though we didn't need another chair.

"Where will it live?" I had asked when he started working on it.

"First you didn't want my bench, and now you don't want my chair." He had sniffed loudly for effect.

"I love your bench, and I will love your chair. But . . . " I hesitated and looked at him apologetically.

"But what?"

"Well, you know." I broke eye contact and stared intently at the floor.

"Know what, Jana? My wife, my love, my life partner, my best friend?" His voice rose dramatically with each term, though laughter hid behind his words. "What were you going to say?"

"We haven't used your bench," I blurted. "We haven't used it since the first morning that it was ready and you wanted us to do coffee time on the front porch to 'honor the occasion', or whatever you said. We haven't used it, and it's just sitting there."

He inhaled sharply through flared nostrils and sucked in his lips. "And there. It. Is. You hate my furniture."

I laughed openly then, knowing it was what he wanted. "I love your furniture. I love it so much that I want to make sure it's used. I only wondered where we would put the table because I wanted to make sure it would get all the love and use it deserves."

"We'll find a place for it," he answered easily, his show of hurt feelings set aside for the moment. "Maybe on the front porch."

I arched an eyebrow.

"What?" he asked. "Even if we don't use it, you have to admit the bench gives the porch character."

"Sure, sure." And he plowed ahead with his plans for a chair, and I tried not to be bothered wondering whether it would match the rest of our furniture or have a suitable place in our home.

I thought about that conversation as I sipped my martini again and watched Michael muse about his table, thought about how much he made me laugh, how generous and kind he was, how he never minded that I could be uptight, and I tried to stop being annoyed with him.

He was going through his own things, too. He was less and less interested in his normal work, and seemed to resent having his focus torn from his volunteer work. He'd been spending long nights helping design an online educational program that would be offered to students in junior high and high schools that didn't have the resources to offer wide-ranging electives or advanced classes. He was more passionate about it than I'd ever seen him about a paying job. It was understandable that he wouldn't be able to devote all his attention to easing every fear I had.

Oh, and there's that little matter of his new wife, the woman he's known and loved for several years and never once mistreated, thinking he might be a psycho. That'll cause anyone some stress...

"It does look like it might storm." Michael had wandered to the kitchen window where he stood munching his apple. "So not the best weather for building furniture. Especially since we know how drafty that workshop is."

Suddenly I wanted to slap him. I imagined chucking my glass right across the room and watching it bounce off his temple. He so casually alluded to my ruined table like it was nothing more than a funny little memory. So much for not being annoyed with him.

"Do you want to watch a movie or something instead?" he asked, oblivious to my rage, which I swallowed with my martini, and set both aside with determination.

Stop being so sensitive. You're being ridiculous.

With how easily Michael let things go and how rare it was for him to stay angry about anything, it probably didn't occur to him that I was still nursing an open wound about my table.

I hadn't realized until he offered for us to spend the evening together how much I had been dreading settling into my usual comfortable spot on the couch to read. The activity was tainted by the memory of someone covering me with a blanket and whispering in my ear. I forced a smile, relieved not to be left alone. I was, in spite of everything, in spite of his cavalier reference to my table, happy to spend time with him. Happy to keep him by my side, to avoid facing the long dark walk down the hall to our bedroom alone.

I wondered if he sensed my need.

"That sounds good," I said.

I led the way to the living room, drink in hand.

Though maybe I don't need it anymore, if we go to bed together.

Things were less confusing when we went to bed at the same time. At least then I knew our conversations were real. I sipped the drink anyway though, with the enjoyment now of someone drinking for pleasure rather than need, and settled myself on the couch, leaning against him.

As he began looking for something to watch, asking me for input that I gave without thought, almost automatically—no, I looked that up recently and the ratings were terrible; maybe, it looks kind of funny; no, nothing suspenseful tonight—I continued to sip and watch him.

I met his parents shortly after I met him, and I loved them. Or did I love their life? Happy marriage; family of college-educated, stable people; two children who talked almost daily even as adults living in different states. Vacation homes and retirement plans. It made sense that we would have those things, too. He had to want them. But I couldn't remember if I'd actually asked.

I was sure I had. We had talked about having children. The importance of a strong marriage. Planning for our future. All things I pretended weren't entirely foreign to me and that were certainly natural to him.

What would he have to gain by lying to me about the dreams? It was silly to suspect him. And when I considered everything he would have had to do to pull off such elaborate deceit, it was laughable.

He was Michael. My Michael. Simple, straightforward, undemanding Michael.

***

The nightmares returned that night. Returned or continued, I wasn't sure if I could say. I was sleeping on my side as usual, on the edge of the bed closest to the bedroom door, my back to Michael's side, when the door flew open and Michael strode into the room with determination, kneeling in front of me and taking my hand.

"You have to get up," he said urgently. My heart thudding, I allowed him to pull me from the bed and lead me from the room.

I didn't look behind me. I was dazed and half asleep and I didn't think to check Michael's side of the bed. I still wonder, if I had looked behind me, what I would have seen.

"What's going on?" I asked when we reached the hallway, but he continued pulling me forward without a word. We reached the living room, shrouded in dim moonlight, and he stopped and looked around.

"I heard something outside," he whispered. A chill ran over my skin, raising the hair on my legs and arms, and I held his hand tighter.

"What was it?" I asked.

"I don't know."

"What are we doing?"

"Waiting." He stood stock-still, facing the window, his head turned away from me.

"For what?" I hadn't had time to grab my robe and was wearing only a short cotton nightgown, barefoot and shivering.

"Shh." He squeezed my hand before letting it go, and crossed to the back door. I stood, confused and helpless and tired, in the middle of the living room; the dark kitchen loomed to one side and the staircase rose into blackness on the other, but I didn't suggest turning on the light, knowing he was trying to see into the yard.

"I thought I saw someone pass by our window," he said, speaking over his shoulder. "I need you to stay right here on the couch so I can see if anything happens." He turned and closed the distance between us in a few quick steps, grabbing my hand and leading me to the couch. I sat numbly, wanting to protest.

"What about my phone?" I started to rise and go back to the bedroom to get it, but he lifted his hand.

"Hold on," he said. Before I could protest further, he darted to the back door and looked out and then, to my surprise, he opened the door and was gone even as I yelped, "Michael! What are you doing? Get back here!"

I crossed quickly to the door and locked it behind him and turned on the back porch light, ready to open the door again in a flash if Michael appeared. He was already out of sight. My breath was coming in short inhales that I couldn't seem to let out again, my chest pulsing, my nostrils flared, my eyes wide and searching. It was a black, starless night that swallowed the weak rays cast by the porch light, and I could see nothing past a few feet of brightness. Our workshop was enveloped in darkness; I squinted at it and tried to make out something, anything, in the darkness. I thought I saw a figure moving behind it, but in the deep purple-black night, I couldn't tell if it was real.

I had no idea where he had gone and couldn't believe he would leave me defenseless, with not even my phone nearby, with a possible intruder outside our house. What kind of person rushes unarmed into the night after a stranger who might be dangerous? His behavior was erratic, completely unlike himself.

I don't know how long I stayed there, pinned to the door, staring into the night. My feet were numb with cold before I shifted and exhaled, resolving to go to the bedroom for my phone. I wasn't sure if Michael had his with him, but if I couldn't find him, I needed to call the police.

Suddenly it hit me that Holly wasn't in her place, and the fear already pressing on my chest grew heavier. If something had happened to her, then the danger was very real.

III

"Holly," I let out a loud whisper. She hadn't been in the living room with us and she hadn't gone out with him. If she had been nearby, she would have leapt from her bed to greet Michael, as she did any time he entered a room, and she would have stayed by his side. "Holly?" I said again, wondering if Michael put her outside before he heard whatever noise it was that set the night's events in motion.

A movement on the staircase almost made me scream until I recognized the tap of Holly's paws and saw her appear shortly after. I didn't pause to wonder why she hadn't been in her usual spot, or why she'd stayed away upstairs while Michael and I were in the living room; the confusion flew through my mind and was set aside in an instant. Michael had been gone for several minutes now and I needed to do something. Emboldened by my ninety-pound defense, I ran down the hall with Holly on my heels, picturing the intruder ready to leap from the hall closet or guest room doors, imagining coming face to face with him when I reached the bedroom, ready to shove, punch, kick, headbutt, and anything else I needed to do to get to my phone and get help, and I burst into the bedroom.

But there was no intruder there.

Only Michael. Sleeping soundly.

CHAPTER NINETEEN

"**COULD YOU COME** to my office when you have a minute?"
The instant message was laying in wait for me when I turned on my screen first thing in the morning, its ominous flash like a shout that things were already wrong, much too early in the day. But lately, I woke up every day feeling like things were wrong.

Like "we need to talk" and "with all due respect", a random summoning to the boss's office first thing in the morning was a bad omen, but I wasn't sure I could bring myself to care much that morning. I only sighed and blinked at the screen, my shoulders slumping a little further in defeat, and rubbed my eyes in circular motions that spread to my aching temples. I was relieved that I hadn't bothered with makeup that morning and could wipe the sleep from my eyes freely.

There was no good explanation for the night before. It was ridiculous to seriously consider that Michael had gone out the back door, through the yard, in through the bedroom window, and under the covers...but I did. I had woken Michael up before I left for work and asked if we could check the security footage from the night before, making up a story about hearing strange noises in the back yard while watching him closely for any sign that he was nervous about the request. But after some standard grumbling about being woken up, he went to the computer without argument.

Only the footage wasn't there. The moment played over and over in my brain as I finished getting ready for work, during my morning commute, as I walked through the building giving automated responses to coworkers' greetings—Michael's face turning from his computer, smooth of worry or concern, and telling me, "Oh, I forgot to finish setting up the hard drive. I had it so we could view the live feed, but it hasn't been saving the footage this whole time. My bad. What do you think you heard?"

A few months ago, I would have thought nothing of an oversight like that. Michael could be infuriatingly absent-minded. How many times had I followed one of his trails of half-opened cabinets and drawers through the house, or found refrigerated food left out on the counter to spoil, or had to finish an abandoned house project for him because he had gotten distracted? Under normal circumstances, this would be standard Michael.

But things were different now. I wasn't going to rush to accusations though, allowing him to make me look like a fool again.

And I could have been sleepwalking. It had to be considered.

Or crazy.

It had to be considered.

Was he there in bed behind me? Was it something else entirely that burst into our bedroom? A ghost? Do I even believe in ghosts? Why, why didn't I turn my head to look?

I sighed again at Devin's message. It was the last thing I wanted to deal with that morning, but I couldn't ignore it.

"Have a seat," Devin said easily when I came into his office. There may have been a flicker of surprise that darted across his face at my appearance, or maybe I imagined it. If I looked even a fraction as disordered as I felt, I couldn't make a good impression. "I wanted to talk to you about moving around some client assignments," he said.

"Okay," I said, neutral.

"I saw that Mr. Worthing asked to add the new AI tool and some other additional fraud monitoring services across his companies. Great job on introducing him to those options."

And the other shoe . . . ?

"Thank you," I said.

"No, thank you," he said it like a correction. "But we were thinking; since the tool is so new to the firm and Julieta took the lead on implementing it with the first client, and she has the most experience with it, it'd probably make sense to shift Mr. Worthing to her team."

There it is. Julieta. Smart, capable, and always poised. Her heels were never less than three inches tall, and her eyes were never, ever fit for rubbing, as that would mar subtle but perfectly applied eye shadow, liner, and mascara. Things that had all been true of me a few short months ago.

"I'm confident my team can handle it," I said, hoping I sounded diplomatic and assured rather than argumentative. "I would be happy to bring Julieta in as needed, when we need her expertise."

"I know you can," Devin agreed quickly. "But we need you in another way. We'd like to do a switch so that you take three of Julieta's team's smaller clients instead." Devin said "we" as though it wasn't his sole decision. "So you'll actually be gaining a couple of clients." He shared it like an exciting announcement, like a favor, like a reward. "I know you can handle it."

More work for less money, you mean. The extra time spent on emails, meetings, communication, and other repeated processes made three small clients far less lucrative than one large one. Not to mention that Mr. Worthing was surprisingly undemanding for a client of that size, and that his was a name I could put on my personal client list and it would get a prospective client's attention. I doubted the same could be said of the clients Julieta was getting rid of.

"That's great," I lied. "I'm happy to meet with Mr. Worthing and Julieta to make it a smooth transition."

"Perfect. If you could get that scheduled, that would be great."

And of course I'm the one scheduling things. Next thing I know he'll be asking me to bring in some snacks, too. He gave me a brilliant smile that told me we were done.

I walked back to my office, not sure if I wanted to cry or throw up. I slumped at my desk and stared at my computer in a daze. It felt like I'd just been punished for upselling a client.

I tried to rationalize, tried to be okay with it, tell myself that he was such an important client that it would be a bad idea to learn a new service with him. That it was all for the best.

But the image that kept replaying in my head was Julieta walking into Charles Jacob Worthing V's office like she owned it and having no doubts about her right to be there. I kicked myself for not doing a better job at defending my case.

Or any job. You didn't fight for it at all. You smiled and you took it lying down.

I wondered if the me from a few months ago would have taken it. The me who wasn't questioning my marriage, my sanity, or my grip on reality. Maybe that version of myself wouldn't be put in that situation to begin with.

The day dragged from there. I spent my time half-focused, expecting Julieta to pop in my office at any moment to talk about the transition. I expected she would be bright and matter-of-fact about it, pretending it wasn't a slight in any way. When the hours rolled by and she didn't appear, I began to be annoyed that she hadn't.

Did she expect me to come to her? Or was she planning to contact Mr. Worthing without talking to me first?

My stomach clenched and the blood rushed to my cheeks at the thought of her sidestepping my role entirely and inserting herself without acknowledging the relationship I helped build.

Okay, I'm being ridiculous. I breathed deeply and remembered it hadn't even been a full day since I got the news, and there was no rush for the transition to happen. She might not even be working in the office that day.

"Did your husband find you?" a male voice interrupted.

The question startled me into dropping my pen with a clatter as Lex, one of our interns, poked his head into my office.

"What?" I asked.

"Your husband. I thought I saw him walk by the breakroom. He looked a little lost." He hesitated as he took in my blank, confused expression. "Maybe it wasn't him," he said. "I only met him the one time, at the happy hour. Maybe it was someone that looked like him."

"Oh, it could be him," I scrambled for a response as my heart began to pound. "Sometimes he drops in."

He had dropped in exactly one time before, to surprise me with a plant for my new office and to take me for a celebratory lunch marking the close of my first week with the firm. It was late afternoon, almost time to leave for the day, so lunch couldn't be the explanation.

"Or maybe it is someone else; he does have one of those faces," I said with a laugh. I reached for my phone and hesitated.

What would I say? "Are you here?" What if he wasn't? Wouldn't that make me sound paranoid? I could blame Lex, of course, but with everything . . .

Lex laughed awkwardly and seemed unsure if there was a mystery he was supposed to help me solve, or if he could leave.

"I'll message him and find out," I told him with a reassuring smile, and he left. I picked up my phone and typed out the message, "Are you in my building?"

And then I stared at it. If he wasn't there, if Lex was mistaken, I'd sound insane texting him something like that.

"Did you stop by my work?" I typed instead, hoping it sounded more casual. My thumb hovered over the 'send' icon, but still I hesitated.

"Hey!" Michael's sudden appearance startled me into dropping my phone with another clatter.

"Shit!" I said involuntarily.

"Nice to see you too," he said, looking surprised and a little amused at my reaction, and maybe pleased with himself for making me jump.

"Sorry. I was about to message you," I said, rising and walking around my desk to give him a quick kiss in greeting. "One of the interns thought he saw you here, and I was confused. What are you doing here?" I was careful to ask the last question lightly and like my surprise was a pleasant one.

"I came by because my phone died this morning," he said. "Permanently. It's a goner."

"Oh no!" The exclamation was sympathetic, but I switched to being playful and followed up with, "What did you do to it?"

It felt forced, trying to joke around, though he didn't seem to notice.

"Sometimes phones just die, you know," Michael answered.

"Uh huh," I said. "Sure they do."

"There may have been a coffee incident. That's beside the point. The point is, I considerately came over here in person to let you know that I will be going to the store and can't be reached for a while. Also, probably going to swing by Luke's house since it's in the area, so I might not be home when you get off," he said, and added with all the piousness he could muster, "Your office is a full fifteen minutes out of my way, but I didn't want you to worry."

I laughed at him. "That's very kind of you. I'm sorry about your phone."

"It's fine. How's your day going?"

I hesitated, wanting to tell him about my client, but seeing also that he already had one foot out of my office, eager to pick out an upgrade for his coffee-drenched phone.

"It's good," I said. *I'll tell him later.*

His hand on the doorframe, he leaned back into the office to kiss me on the cheek.

"I'll see you when you get home," I said. "I love you."

"Love you, too."

***

The driveway was empty when I arrived home, as expected. It was one of those evenings when night descended without warning: an early dusk of orange and pink when I left the office, nothing but a fast-disappearing sliver of light breaking the darkness by the time I got home.

I got out of my car and walked up the drive of stones arranged like hopscotch and flanked by somber green plants that would stay flowerless for at least another month until spring came, and maybe longer. Spring was a tease in our area; we would get a taste of it as early as February and have frost again as late as May. I tried not to make eye contact with the windows that stared out at me so expressionlessly. Without the knowledge of Michael being inside to keep it warm and lit, the house became a foreign, unwelcoming thing.

I opened the door and the groan of its hinges was followed swiftly by the tap of claws scraping against the hardwood floors, and then a dark mass moving toward me. I almost stepped back out the door before recognizing that it was only Holly coming to greet me. Her tail wagged slowly, pleased to see me, if not a little half-hearted about it in comparison to her overjoyed reactions to Michael's every arrival.

"Oh, hi." I bent to scratch her ears. "Did you check the house for monsters for me? Did you?" She leaned lazily into my busy fingers moving along her neck. "Or did you lie here and invite them to wait in the drawing room? It seems like something you'd do." Talking out loud didn't help make the house feel less imposing.

I moved through the entryway toward the living room, unconsciously giving the dark hallway a wide berth, glancing reluctantly at the gaping mouth leading into nothing. My hand darted out into the void and flipped the hall switch, flooding it with welcome light, and I let out my breath. I hesitated where I stood. To my right, the hall, with its many doors; doors into bedrooms and bathrooms and closets, bedrooms with dark spaces behind more closets, bathrooms with dark spaces behind shower curtains. Directly in front of me, the living room, with its line of windows gaping toothlessly out at the night. Or in at me. The back door leading to the porch. I wondered if Michael had remembered to lock it before he left. And of course, a few steps in front of me and to the right, the stairwell.

My home held so many places to hide.

My mind went back to the prior night, standing in that same spot, watching Michael dart to the window and then out the back door. It was all so surreal.

Holly stood as a statue beside me for a while before, perceiving that no more scratches were forthcoming, she trotted back to her spot in the living room, climbed onto the couch, and curled into a ball.

The living room it would be, made safer by her presence. I followed her, glancing behind me as I put my back to the cavernous opening of the hallway. For a split second before I looked, I could see the image in my mind of someone, something, taking the opportunity to leap from the shadows; it flashed so clearly that I flinched when I looked, despite seeing nothing there.

I tried to remember the last time I'd been home without Michael, at night, and realized it hadn't happened in at least the past year, maybe longer. I had never been alone in that house for more than the time it took Michael to go on a quick grocery run or workout.

I settled on the couch next to Holly, reached for the remote, and paused with it in my hand, listening. Holly's ears remained perked and she sat frozen, facing the entryway that branched down the hallway, now flooded with light, but hidden from my point of view from the couch.

My mind wandered. If someone did come into our house while we were gone and laid in wait in a shadowy corner until we were home, which corner would they choose? They could probably move from one of the bedrooms or closets into the hallway without my hearing them.

If they were standing just around the corner, would I know it? Would I hear him breathing?

The moment I thought it, I began to think I did hear breathing, so soft it might be a breeze, and I held my own, listening intently.

Holly hadn't moved. Her eyes stayed locked on the living room doorway.

In spite of my reluctance to turn from the exposed entrance that Holly inexplicably felt so inclined to guard, I had the sudden need to look behind me, where the back door loomed and gaping windows stared uncovered into the back yard. As I turned my head in a quick, darting motion, panic took its place beside me and I knew something was going to come from the hallway. I glanced at the door behind me for only a second before snapping back to the entryway, but there was nothing there.

I scanned the empty room and my gaze traveled back to Holly, who I saw with a sickening wave of dread was no longer staring at the hallway.

Her eyes were fixed on the space above and behind me.

I know that means nothing. I will look and there will be nothing there.

I whirled and let out a stifled shriek when something brushed across my face before realizing it was my own hair. I was alone in the room except for Holly, no one standing over my shoulder. I looked at Holly and at the space behind me again, tracing the invisible line to where her eyes had been resting.

The small window in the back door, black and impassive. My skin prickled again, and I reached for the back porch light switch. The switch had been buggy since we installed the new motion detectors, and nothing happened when I flipped it.

"Shit," I muttered to Holly. She seemed to take it as an invitation, and she hopped from the couch and trotted to the back door, where she sat down in front of it and stared expectantly. She wanted out. I squinted at the black square that was the window, useless in the dark night. I didn't want to open the door without being able to look first.

"Damn motion detectors."

Holly shifted impatiently and whined.

"I know, I know." I bit my lip and considered. "And I know the light would turn on if someone was out there. Theoretically."

Unless someone planned ahead and removed the bulbs . . .

"Oh, I do know. I'll turn off all the lights in here, and then maybe I'll be able to see into the back yard. And then I can let you out." As I narrated my thoughts, Holly tilted her head and continued staring at me, unimpressed. I went to the kitchen first, then the entryway, turning off lights as I went. When I turned off the hallway light, transforming it back into a black tunnel I couldn't see the end of, I shuddered and fled back to Holly where she waited like a statue.

And I looked into the dark. I concentrated until my eyes ached, but all I could see was the outline of the wooden beams supporting the roof over the porch, and beyond those, the white and gray workshop stood out like a beacon in the darkness. No intruder, no movement, no strange shapes.

"I am a crazy person," I muttered to Holly. "How did I get here?" Nose pressed against the glass, searching for shadows, next to a longsuffering dog with a full bladder.

How had I allowed myself to devolve so far? *We are the children of addicts who were each batshit crazy in their own special ways.* Ivy's words echoed in my head, spoken shortly after she moved to St. Louis. *We have to do better. We have to face what we are.*

What Ivy is, not me, I had thought at the time, not wanting to admit even to myself that I was thinking it, that I was taking a mental step away from her, drawing a line, separating myself from her. I never even tried drugs and rarely drank in college. I saw a therapist when our mother died as a purely preventive measure, and I chose a life partner I trusted and respected. I was not her, I told myself, and definitely not our mother. I didn't have to be crazy.

How did I get here?

I investigated people for a living. Not in the most exciting way, through numbers and spreadsheets and computer software, but it was what I did. And there I was, frozen by suspicion and paranoia, unwilling to open closet doors in my own home. I made a decision. I straightened my back and turned from the back door and went up the stairs to Michael's office, Holly close behind me. If he wasn't the person I thought he was, there would be a sign. There were always signs, when anyone bothered to look.

I didn't have my own computer at home. I frequently brought my work computer home, so I hadn't gotten around to replacing my last personal computer after it had died a couple years ago. I used Michael's when I needed one and didn't have my work computer handy; he always told me I was welcome to use it any time. In fact, he referred to it as "our" computer.

But I still felt like an intruder as I crept softly across the office carpet and sat at his desk. The chair was too high, the back support leaning too far forward, as if to tell me I had no place there, and I didn't dare adjust them. I was allowed to be in here, I told myself.

It's the "why" you're here that's the problem though, isn't it?

I moved his mouse, expecting to be stymied at the first screen when a password request popped up—I was no hacker—but his unlocked desktop appeared before me instead.

Nothing to hide.

Holly had positioned herself on the floor behind me instead of her usual spot beneath Michael's desk, and it felt like a rejection. A reprimand, even. My feet were not the right ones to lie at. I shrugged away the guilt and opened his browser. That wasn't where I'd start with a client; usually, my investigations started with reviewing and analyzing the reports they supplied me.

But this wasn't a client, and I would be crazy not to start with the obvious. I went straight for the browser history.

I don't know what I expected to find. "How to prank your wife in new and exciting ways" seemed unlikely to appear, but there had to be something, somewhere. When people create a false persona, when people have a secret, when they're hiding dark and twisted things, there are traces. Like Evelyn and her generous Christmas gifts. Like the HR manager with odd web searches about pregnancy. No one should have needed to open a financial report to figure out they were hiding things.

Michael's most recent searches related to his phone—of course. He had searched for locations and hours of the nearest store, and before that he had watched a video of how to take apart a phone of his model and clean it. Before all the phone-related searches, there was a stream of work-related sites listed, so he must have been working when he broke the phone. There were various social media and news sites interspersed between his work searches throughout the day.

"What are you doing?" asked Michael suddenly, and I smothered my impulse to scream.

"How do I view the feed from the security cameras?" I was amazed at how quickly the deceit came to me.

"Oh, on the computer," he said, his face clearing. "Do you need me to show you again? Did you see something?"

"No, nothing happened. I just wanted to adjust the settings for the cameras and the motion detectors. I couldn't see anything on the camera because the light wouldn't come on. I'm not sure if they're set to only come on when there's motion? I wanted to change it so it would come on any time I flipped the switch."

"Oh," he said, looking troubled. "I'm not sure, but I can look into it."

"Okay." I pushed away from his computer, having closed the browser the moment he arrived, leaving his regular, unassuming desktop behind.

"Did something happen? To make you need the motion detector light?"

"Well, Holly wanted out, and I just wanted to be able to look over the back yard before I opened the door. I guess I got freaked out being here without you."

"Oh." He crossed the room and laid his jacket on the back of his chair. "I guess I'll just never leave you again."

That seems extreme.

Holly whined insistently at his feet.

"Wait, so Holly hasn't been out since you got home?" he asked.

"No." I hated to admit it. "I'm sorry. Like I said, the back porch light wouldn't come on, so I couldn't look out there, and I . . . I don't know, I was being stupid."

He began walking away before I finished talking, striding quickly to the stairs, talking over his shoulder. "Jana, I've been gone for hours. It's already more than she's used to. You can't just ignore our dog's basic needs because you're 'freaked out'." He used quotes with his fingers, mocking me again, and I defended myself as I followed him down the stairs.

"I was not ignoring her needs. I got distracted, I was going to let her out when I was finished."

"Fine." He flung the door open without sparing so much as a glance into the yard first, unconcerned and unafraid, and Holly rushed through.

Somehow, his irritation seemed another point in his favor, as though loving his dog meant he had to be the Michael I thought he was; as though lying to me would mean he wouldn't have the nerve to get upset with me. As though I didn't really know at all what humans are capable of.

CHAPTER TWENTY

I **DON'T KNOW** when I started drinking more than I should have. It was a gradual slip. A few nights of indulgence, followed by a step back. After the sleepwalking incident when I found myself in the living room waiting for a nonexistent intruder, I stopped drinking for a week. Then, after a week filled with hazy nighttime conversations and kisses in the dark I didn't want to ask about, another slip. I had fewer memories the nights I drank; a strong drink before bed meant a dreamless sleep.

But I still woke up tired. With no sense of peace. And the thought began to bloom in the back of my mind, a question about those blank nights of deadened sleep.

Do I not dream those nights, or do I not remember my dreams?

"What do you mean?" Ivy asked me a few days later, when I let the thought slip through my lips in a moment of careless musing. We were sitting across from each other in the tiny kitchen that adjoined Ivy's bookshop.

Shit.

I tried to remember exactly what I said and how I said it. I knew I had been talking about not having the dreams every night and wondering if they were still happening without me. I realized when she looked at me in confusion that it was an odd way to talk about dreams; but not too crazy, I hoped.

Ivy began talking again before I had a chance. "What's the difference between dreams happening and not remembering them, and not having the dream at all?"

"I don't know. Never mind."

I had told her about the night I thought Michael dragged me to the living room, though I tried to downplay the drama of it. I hadn't told Michael about it and it felt strange, sharing something with Ivy and needing her to keep it from him, but she had reacted in her typical nonjudgmental way. I'd told her vaguely about the dreams continuing for a few days after that, and I'd told her about not trusting my dreamless nights. I hadn't mentioned the drinking, of course. With her history, there was no way she could be objective about that, no way she couldn't overreact. But somehow now, I had fallen into dangerous territory.

"Jana, be real. You keep talking about all this like it's silly little dreams, but you're not acting like it. Do you think something is really happening?" she asked.

I laughed, wanting nothing more than to chase away that look on my sister's face: a look of uncertainty about whether she wanted to keep asking about something when the answer might reveal unpleasantness; a fissure in the stable foundation of our lives, the happiness of which was so closely intertwined with rationality, depending so wholly on our escape from a world of anxiety and paranoia and distress.

"What do you think is happening, Mom?" the question echoed in my mind. I don't know how old we were when we stopped asking *"What happened?"* because she wasn't a credible source to tell us. *What do you think happened?*

Such a subtle change, but she was only capable of giving her own unreliable interpretation of the world around her. Out of all the things we might hear from her, what actually happened was unlikely to be one of them.

"All that's happening," I said, "is that I keep having messed up dreams." I had to say it, and in the brightness of her cheerful kitchen, I almost believed myself.

I met her eyes with a smile before adding in what I hoped was a clearly facetious tone, "Or I'm being haunted, or stalked by a psycho, or Michael has an evil twin who he was separated from at birth and he tracked us down, eager to reunite, only instead he spied on us from afar to learn our habits and then thought hey, I could have some fun first."

"Ooh, a Michael twin, that's some creepy shit. I like that," Ivy said, no longer worried, allowing herself to play along now that she knew she wasn't indulging dangerous delusions. She raised her feet, shoeless and clad in mismatched socks, and tucked them under herself in her seat, arranging her bright green, asymmetrical fairy skirt over her legs.

"Well, as long as you're getting some entertainment out of it," I said, forcing a grin. "But anyway, enough about my weird dreams. What's new with you?"

I was beginning to feel an imbalance in our relationship, the focus of every recent conversation being on me. Michael's words came back to me again. *You're not the only one who's allowed to have problems, Jana.*

"Oh, same shit as usual. I told you I started hosting an Audiobooks & Yoga class in the extra space out back, right?"

"You did; how's that going?"

"It's great. I think so, anyway. The try-hard yogis are saying listening to a book while you do yoga defeats the purpose and doesn't allow you to get all centered and shit but whatever. We have earplugs if you need the hour to be about clearing your mind. Some people practice for the physical benefits and can't handle not getting more out of that time. If listening to a book makes them feel like the time isn't wasted, I say it's worth it for them."

"That makes sense to me." It was easy for me to agree. Spending an hour in silent contemplation was never something I was good at. "What else have you had going on?"

She hesitated, and my attention grew. I had only been making small talk, but now I saw there was something else she wanted to share and was nervous. Ivy was rarely nervous.

"I've been painting more lately," she said.

"That's wonderful," I said, but my guard was up now. If she was nervous to share her painting with me, it had to be something she knew I wouldn't like. Where I handled pain and bad memories by trying to forget them, Ivy confronted them with a sledgehammer. I began imagining the scenes I had described to her: Michael sitting on the edge of the bed, Michael holding my hand in the living room, Michael hovering over me while I napped. If I had to see any one of those things represented on a canvas, I wasn't sure what I would do. My heart was thudding and though I lifted my mug smoothly to my lips without betraying my fear, I was terrified to see what she had painted.

She gazed at me for a moment, contemplating, before making a sudden decision. "You might not like it," she warned me, rising from her chair and darting to the other room.

With that, I was certain I would not. She returned with a large canvas pressed against her chest with the back toward me, then flipped it when she stood before me, balancing it against her knee as she turned it carefully.

I saw a middle-aged woman lying in her bed beneath a storm cloud filled with monsters and shadows, oversized spiders, ghouls, and bony, long-fingered hands reaching toward her, grasping and clutching. The cloud of horror took up most of the painting, but on the edge, hovering in the background in the doorway, were two small girls, painted in soothing colors of blues and grays that contrasted sharply with the vivid reds and blacks of the cloud.

It was not what I expected, and I wondered if it was worse. My eyes filled with tears the moment I saw it. In a moment, I was back in that house, back in that doorway, staring at our mother and wondering if it was safe to bother her and tell her how long it had been since we had eaten. I was holding Ivy's hand again, feeling the pressure of her fingers against my palm, and hoping she would take the first step forward.

She always did. And sometimes it was fine. Mom would shake herself, mumble about not being able to get any sleep because of our nagging, but she would make her way to the kitchen anyway. Cranky, but controlled. Or she would tell us what we could make ourselves and roll back over. As far back as I could remember, she had had wild theories and fears about our food. That it could be compromised somehow, that the government lied about expiration dates, that it could be poisoned; she would take one look at a loaf of bread or a gallon of milk that she had just brought home the day before and she would dump the milk down the drain or throw the bread away in the trash outside where we couldn't get to it.

I don't know how old we were when we figured it out and stopped asking her what was safe to eat.

I wanted nothing more than for Ivy to take the painting away, to turn it around, to cover it and hide it and never show it to me again and hopefully, preferably, never show it to another living soul, because I couldn't bear to think of anyone else in the whole world laying their eyes on something so intimate. I looked down, unable to meet Ivy's gaze, unable to pretend I was okay with her creation. She set it down carefully on a chair, facing away from me.

"I should've known you wouldn't like it," she said. I was surprised to hear a hint of judgment in her tone, and I knew she was hurt.

I didn't say I didn't like it.

The words hovered behind my lips but didn't come. I knew I was supposed to correct and reassure her, but I couldn't push the words out. I realized I was not only saddened by the image and disturbed to see our mother's mental illness (and our own selves as children shown afraid and always second, always in the background) put on display and dragged out into the light—I was saddened and disturbed by these things, but I realized I was also angry. Angry that she thought it her right to reveal that which was equally mine.

"I'm sorry," I said. "You know I don't see the point of dwelling on those things."

"Do you really not dwell, though? Because I think you do."

Every once in a while, Ivy's normally compassionate, relaxed nature was interrupted in a flash of temper, and when that happened, her usual bluntness—a quality she valued much more highly than I ever had—veered into harshness. I stiffened, knowing she would have more to say.

"It isn't healthy to bury everything and pretend it doesn't exist, Jana. I work very hard to actually deal with my bullshit, and we have a lot of bullshit. You try so hard to pretend everything is fine, and it's made you uptight and incapable of having a basic fucking conversation about our past."

It was like being doused in rage. *Your painting is hideous*, I wanted to say. *It's a pathetic cry for attention, and maybe you live in the past because it's your excuse for having your history and being where you are and never getting any further. But unlike you, I can control myself.*

With infinite calm, I set down my coffee mug and stood up.

Ivy groaned in loud frustration. "See, you can't even talk to me right now! You're just going to walk away and bury this, too."

"I am not going to fight with you," I said. "My life is really good right now." The words sounded hollow in my ears. "And the things you put in that painting are very personal."

"Art *is* personal."

I refrained from rolling my eyes.

"Jana, you act like our mom having problems is the most shameful thing imaginable."

I scoffed at the idea of describing her conditions as "having problems", and Ivy barreled forward.

"You've never once let me talk to you about the fact that we need to take extra care of ourselves, that our risks—"

"I take care of it," I interrupted, unable to bear letting her continue.

"Fine, if you say so."

"I'm sorry I don't feel the same way you do about it," I said. It was all I could manage.

Ivy's flash of anger was gone as quickly as it came, resignation settling in its place. "I didn't mean to start a fight," she said. "I just wanted to tell you about a stupid local art contest I entered. My painting was a finalist."

"That's great. I'm happy for you."

All I could think about was how many people must have seen the painting in order to judge and rank and award it, but I swallowed my anger.

All I wanted was to enjoy the life I'd worked so very hard to build for myself. For that brief moment, Ivy's painting felt as big a threat to that life as everything else that was happening.

Chapter Twenty-One

EVERYTHING CHANGED A few nights later.

The night it happened, I was reading in the living room as night fell. Michael had been working all evening, and an eerie silence had descended on the house.

Though I tried to focus on my book, pricking at my consciousness were the memories of the last time I'd fallen asleep in that very room, and the whispers in my ear and the blanket I did not cover myself with.

I didn't kiss myself on the cheek and whisper in my own ear.

A chill ran through me and I shuddered, and I longed for Michael's arms around me. Despite my suspicions, I craved everything about the person I still hoped he was, and missed the warm, comfortable light of his office. That office was never silent, filled with the soft hum of his computer and his perpetual typing and clicking. On cool nights, he would light a fire. The stillness in the blank, empty living room was oppressive by comparison. I tossed my book aside and went to find him.

After more than a year into living in that house, we were in some ways still getting settled in. It was my first home, and I didn't know what to do with it. Most of the house was clean and bare and white. But Michael's office was lived-in. There was a change from the rest of our house to that room, and when I went up the stairs and passed through the office door, I transitioned from dim silence into a cheerful, familiar space.

That night, the fire was crackling and warmth ran through me as I shook away the uneasiness that had attached itself downstairs. I crossed the room to lean against him, sitting in his chair, staring at his computer. I nudged my side against his shoulder in greeting and, as usual, in an almost automated response, he snaked his arm around my hips and squeezed without speaking.

Then he looked up at me.

His normally deep, expressive brown eyes were flat and dark. Not Michael's eyes.

He smiled and his teeth were too straight. Not Michael's teeth.

His skin that should have been freckled and flushed was smooth and clear, with a faint grayish sheen.

Stark dread filled me and I stood frozen at his side, looking down into those empty, unfeeling pits. My stomach lurched and I swayed.

He stared at me with a small smile, waiting. *"What will you do?"* his dancing eyes asked.

I gathered myself, cleared my throat, and took a step back.

Will he let me leave?

I walked slowly from the room as he stared after me. When I closed the office door behind me, I fled down the stairs, turning on every light as I went, and stumbled to the couch. I fell into the seat, and I burst into tears. I was facing the bottom of the staircase, watching it, terrified of what might come down. But gradually, as though from a distance, through the panicked ringing in my ears, I became aware of a silence that hadn't been there before, of a noise I hadn't heard until it was gone. It was water flowing through our pipes, turning off.

Michael was in the shower. Michael had been in the shower the entire time. He couldn't have been upstairs, he couldn't have been that thing. How did I miss that Holly was not in the office with him?

That thing is not Michael.

I stared at the entrance of our living room where the staircase and the hallway intersected and I waited, waited to see who would appear where, praying for Michael to hurry.

Hoping it would be Michael who appeared.

PART THREE

CHAPTER TWENTY-TWO

"**H**OW ARE THE dreams lately, Jana?" Dr. Goulding began our session, as she always began each session.

"Still better," I said. "Less frequent."

I had been taking the sleeping pills Dr. Goulding prescribed for me, and I had certainly been sleeping better for it. No more dreams, no more nighttime scenes with Michael-not-Michael at all. I could pretend that made it all better, that I believed it was solved. That I wasn't still wondering what happened while I was unconscious. That everything stopped while I slept.

"That's fantastic," she said. "And you haven't had another waking nightmare?" she asked.

"No." I shook my head and pushed a close-mouthed smile across my face. Waking nightmares. That was the rational explanation for the thing I saw.

"Have you been checking in with Michael like we discussed? Confirming whether conversations and interactions are real?"

"Yes, but I haven't had to lately. There haven't been interactions when I'm half asleep, like before. I guess the pills are working." *If being too senseless and comatose to know what might be happening can be called 'working'.*

"That's good." She looked thoughtful for a moment. "Was Michael patient with you when you started checking with him more? I know you were worried about him losing confidence in you."

"He's been great," I said. "We've been better than ever lately. He's thoughtful and sweet, and he comes to bed earlier now, since that seems to help me."

I had known Dr. Goulding for years. I saw her a few times while I was in college, and for a while after my mom died. I hadn't seen her in a couple of years, but after the office incident, Michael and I decided I would go again.

"I know that having a parent with the problems your mother had makes your own mental state a scary topic," she said. "And makes something even resembling a hallucination very scary. But you display none of the disorganized behavior or other symptoms we normally see with schizophrenia. Sleep-related hallucinations, vivid dreams, waking dreams, and so on; these are all more common than people realize. And they're commonly linked to anxiety or other sleep disorders."

"I know," I said. She had gone over this with me before. "That is a relief."

My eyes drifted to the window.

What am I doing here?

It wasn't that I bought into the idea that everything had been in my head. I wasn't there because I truly thought she held the answers. But it was what Michael wanted. And it seemed irresponsible not to go, with everything that had been happening. And the truth is, I liked Dr. Goulding. She made me feel saner, like even if I did start to turn out like my mom, maybe it would be manageable. That maybe it wouldn't mean losing everything.

So I had been honest with her, mostly. I told her the things I had seen and when they happened. In the back of my mind, I think I hoped she would come up with a psychological reason behind it all. Because that would mean there might be solutions. Treatments, medication, whatever the illness called for.

Yet all she had called for was more sleep.

"Jana?" Dr. Goulding broke my reverie. "Do you want to talk any more about the suspicions you were having about Michael?"

"What else do you want to know?" I asked.

She looked thoughtful for a moment. "I think it's important to explore what aspects of your relationship might make you suspect him in the first place."

"Our relationship is good," I said, trying not to sound defensive. "I think anyone might do a little second-guessing in my position. Having constant, realistic dreams about him . . . Everyone has dreams about their partners that they confuse with reality sometimes. I've heard that a lot of people argue with their spouse in their dreams and wake up angry at them. I have a coworker whose husband had consistent dreams about her cheating on him until he eventually became so convinced that he started checking her phone. He got crazy enough to confront her about it, even though he never found anything, without an ounce of proof or any reason for him to be suspicious, except for a few dreams." I forced myself to stop talking. So much for not sounding defensive. Dr. Goulding didn't interrupt me; she stayed quiet and let me talk myself out. Probably a technique they teach.

She allowed the silence to linger for a moment before she answered. "Do you think," she began slowly, "that it would have been as serious as cheating if the whole thing had been a prank Michael was playing on you?"

"Yes," I said without hesitation. "Maybe worse. It would have been a huge violation of my trust. It would have changed everything I thought I knew about him."

"So that's a significant thing to suspect him of, isn't it?"

"Yes." I took my time thinking of my response. "I guess I thought it might be possible because sometimes Michael is a little careless and doesn't seem to understand why certain things upset me."

"Like what?"

I thought of his reaction to my table being ruined, his jokes about not washing my hair. Then I thought of the night I had seen the thing in his office. I sat there in the living room, in tears, terrified that the wrong Michael would come down the stairs and into the living room to confront me. When Michael finally appeared in the hallway leading from our bedroom and not from the stairs, freshly showered and with Holly closely behind him, the slow trickle of tears sprang into sobs of relief the moment I saw him and knew it was him.

He rushed to the couch and asked what was wrong, was I hurt, what had happened?

"There's something upstairs," I choked out.

"What is it?" He tensed, his face serious and intent, and he shifted sideways from his position of kneeling in front of me so his back was no longer turned to the stairwell.

"I saw someone," I said miserably. "It looked like you, but it wasn't you. He was plasticky and wrong."

Michael stared at me for a moment before rising wordlessly and going up the stairs. A few moments later, his foot hit the bottom step again and he moved toward me, giving his head a slight jerk while his mouth stayed fixed in the same straight line it had been in when he went up.

"There's nothing there," he said. "What do you mean, he was like me? Was he wearing a mask?"

"No. I don't know, I don't think so."

"Jana, what do you think you saw?"

I dropped my head in my hands and took a deep breath before lifting my head and looking at him again. "A lot of weird things have been happening, Michael." I brought up the table again, the blanket, the dreams that didn't feel like dreams.

At the end he just stared at me and ran his hands through his hair. "What are you saying you think is happening, Jana?" he asked.

I hated him a little in that moment. I hated him for needing to be told, needing me to drag the dark edges of my mind into the harsh light for him to stare at naked.

"I've never believed in anything supernatural," I said in a small voice. "But there are a lot of weird things happening. I saw someone up there."

He ran his hand through his hair again, even more agitated, and looked away from me the moment I said the word. He brought his hands to his lips, folded like a prayer, but his eyes were wide and unblinking. "Okay," he said slowly. "I was on the verge of calling the cops because you were telling me a person is in our home, possibly wearing a Michael mask. Which is fucking terrifying." I flinched at the deep exasperation layering his voice as he continued. "But the thing is, I can't call the cops about something supernatural, or about a dream, or about anything else."

Anything else. The words tumbled through my mind. *Like hallucinations*, it whispered back to me.

"Did you see an actual person in our house?" he asked me. "A human person?"

I thought of what I saw. No mask could look like that. I shook my head, hating myself, hating him. "I don't think so."

He let out his breath in a rush and sat heavily down beside me. "Okay," he said. "I didn't even know the dreams were still happening." Accusation in his voice. "How often?"

"I don't know." Hot tears ran through the cold, stale ones sticking on my cheeks. "All the time? A lot. Most nights that you're not in bed with me. Maybe some nights when you are."

"Why wouldn't you tell me that?" He looked hurt, offended, and a little angry.

Why would I? Why would I want you to look at me like this?
"I didn't want . . . I wasn't sure . . . " I shrugged helplessly, not knowing what to say, my throat strangling the words before I could make them.

"What, Jana?" His voice was firm. No nonsense.

It angered me enough to make me straighten and continue. "I didn't want you questioning me."

"Questioning you?" he asked, surprised.

"My mind, I mean. I didn't want you thinking I was...unstable or something."

He barely reacted to this admission, like he couldn't understand what the big deal was. "Why would I think that?"

"Oh, I don't know, because I'm possibly seeing things? Or have crazy theories about a scary monster trying to take your place?" I used air quotes around "scary monster", and he smiled a little. *Tell him the truth. If there was ever a time to tell him it's right now.*

He leaned over and kissed my temple, then wrapped his arms around me and squeezed a little. It felt more patronizing than consoling, but I leaned into him and kissed his cheek in return.

"Do you want to talk to Dr. Goulding about it?" he asked. "See what she thinks."

Yes, that's it; I'll talk to Dr. Goulding first, then tell him. Maybe I have nothing to worry about . . . "Yeah. I can do that."

I stared at Dr. Goulding for a moment as I thought over that conversation.

"Everything," I said, finally. "From getting groped in my sleep to being confused about my dreams to thinking I might have been seeing things, to all my worries about not being able to trust my mind in general. Michael shrugs it away and acts like it's all . . . " I searched for the word. "Silly."

Dr. Goulding looked at me thoughtfully. "Does he act like it's silly or does he genuinely think it's silly?"

I blinked and shifted uncomfortably.

Dr. Goulding gazed at me steadily, patiently. "Maybe he only acts like it's silly," I said, wanting to be fair. "Maybe it's his way of trying to make me feel better. But he also makes jokes sometimes, about things I don't think are funny at all."

"Do you tell him when he jokes about things that bother you?"

I looked away, and that was all the answer she needed. She nodded. "That's an acceptable, normal thing to do, Jana; to tell your partner when a topic bothers you rather than internalizing it. It's healthy to assert yourself."

"Okay. I'll work on it."

"What other reasons has he given you to think he's careless?"

I tried to think of anything significant Michael had done, that I knew he had done, that was willfully dismissive of my feelings, and could think of nothing.

"Maybe I've been too hard on him," I said. "Maybe it was unfair of me to think he could do something like this."

"And how is your relationship now?"

"It's great." I could be honest about that; the therapy was going a long way toward improving our relationship. He had been more thoughtful and considerate, while I was trying to be more forgiving and honest. Mostly. "I see what you're saying. It was irrational of me to suspect Michael." I meant it. The thing in the office had broken whatever paranoia I had toward Michael, made all my suspicions of him lying to me seem silly. He'd been on the other side of the house and I had no reason to blame him anymore, and ever since it happened, I'd felt nothing but guilt over how much I had let myself slip into distrusting someone who hadn't done anything wrong.

"I didn't say irrational," she said, so fast that I wondered if it was some kind of buzz word they were trained to avoid.

My mind began to wander as Dr. Goulding spoke gently—everything she said was said gently—about the importance of trust, boundaries, respect . . . And I sat in numb silence, wondering what I was doing there, how it could possibly help with what I was facing.

CHAPTER TWENTY-THREE

I WOKE TO a hand of bright, glaring red filling my vision.

"Happy Valentine's Day," Michael's voice traveled slowly to my consciousness, and I blinked to see a cupcake hovering in front of my face.

"Oh, wow." My voice was thick with sleep, but I focused enough to see Michael kneeling beside our bed with a red-frosted cupcake in his hand.

"Michael, when did you do this?"

"I wish I could take credit for getting up hours early to bake cupcakes, but I am not that impressive. I bought these on my way home yesterday and hid them from you."

He'd gone into the city the day before to see a friend. I wondered now if that was a ruse.

"Aw, well that's still nice of you. Thank you." I sat up and he handed me the cupcake before I had a chance to put my feet on the floor. "Oh," I said. "Are we having cupcakes for breakfast, then? And breakfast in bed?"

"I already ate two, and I want a third one. You have to eat this one right now to make up for it, or I won't be able to live with myself."

I laughed loudly. "Okay, I'll do it for you. But I at least need something to wash it down."

"I already made coffee. I couldn't carry both and get the door. I'll be right back." He kissed my cheek and I smelled the frosting on his breath, then he darted from the room and left me in bed, grinning like a fool with a cupcake in my hand, listening to Holly's click-clacking following him down the hall and through the house. I marveled at his energy level so early in the morning.

I never knew what to expect from Michael on holidays. He was romantic and fond of big gestures, and no Valentine's Day or birthday was like the last. I hoped he didn't have anything too intense planned for us that day; it was our first Valentine's Day as a married couple, but with everything that had been going on, I found myself dreading anything that would take me out of the house and force me to interact with the outside world. Somehow, the more disturbing things happened to me in that house, the less inclined I was to leave it.

And the more things involving Michael that scare me, the more I want him around . . . My eyebrows drew together at the thought and I stared at my cupcake in silence. Was I stupid to stay?

Michael appeared and I brushed the thought aside and greeted him with a smile. He was balancing two cupcakes in one hand and coffee in the other.

"Michael, I hope you're planning on eating four cupcakes for breakfast because one of those can't be for me. I haven't even eaten my first one."

"Nonsense." He deposited the coffee and one of the cupcakes on my bedside table. Then he circled the bed to his side and plopped down on his stomach beside me, keeping his cupcake balanced carefully in his hand as he rested on his elbows. "Once you eat the first one, you'll understand."

I tried to ignore my concerns about crumbs or frosting getting on the comforter, and turned my attention to my cupcake. I didn't share Michael's weakness for sweets and my stomach rumbled nervously at the idea of something so sugary for breakfast, but I decided to indulge him. I peeled the wrapper and took my first bite, noticing him watching me closely. If we hadn't already been married, I'd be expecting to bite into a ring.

I had to admit, it was the most delicious cupcake I'd tasted, and I told him so after I swallowed.

"Right?" He answered enthusiastically. "Now you get it."

"Well, there's still no way I can eat another one this early."

Without a word, he reached up and smacked the bottom of the half a cupcake I held in my hand so it hit my nose. Icing coated my nose and smeared under my left eye, and the crumbs I had been so carefully catching in my hand hovering beneath the cupcake now spilled over my chest and the comforter that was piled up in my lap.

My mouth dropped and I stared at him in shock. He stared back at me in daring audacity, a smile playing on his lips, eyebrows raised, asking what I would do. Without thinking, I snatched the extra cupcake from my bedside table and hurled it at him, keeping it steady in the palm of my hand until it met his face, wanting to press it into his face and thoroughly cover him. He let out an excited, surprised laugh when he saw it coming and tried to duck, so my cupcake got him on the side of his face and smeared into his ear. He groaned loudly and I was surprised to hear a maniacal laugh escaping me as his face screwed up in disgust at the frosting that filled his ear.

"Oh, that's horrible, that is truly horrible!" he said between laughter as he cocked his head and tried to shake the crumbs from his ear. I should have seen what was going to happen next, but I was too busy laughing at him to take any preventative action as he took the remainder of the cupcake in his hand and pressed it into my chest.

"Michael!" I squealed. "Not the cleavage! Do you know how hard it is to get things out of there?"

With that, he pulled himself from his position lying on his stomach and launched himself at me, wrapping me in a hug and rubbing the side of his frosting-covered face on my face while I giggled uncontrollably and scooped cupcake from my sports bra and tried to lodge it in his other ear. Eventually, his mouth found mine and we stopped struggling and leaned into each other, forgetting about the crumbs and the icing and the mess. We never stopped having sex through all the stress and nightmares, but that morning we were our old selves again. Exploring each other with the morning sunlight spilling through the open window; careless and oblivious.

"What else are we doing today?" I asked him a little while after. His head rested on my stomach and I ran my fingers through his sticky hair as I surveyed the disaster that was our bedroom; cupcake wrappers on the bed and floor, red icing streaking the comforter and ourselves, yellow chunks of cupcake spotting the bed and the floor. "Other than laundry, that is."

"Oh, I have plans," he said. "Many great plans." His voice sounded sleepy and far away.

"Michael! We can't go to sleep. Our room is a mess."

He shook himself and stretched. "Okay, okay. We'll toss everything in the wash and get to the next big event."

"Big event?"

"It's Valentine's Day. You didn't think cupcakes were all, did you?" He propped himself up and leaned over to kiss my nose.

"Of course not. I got you something, too."

"You better have." He touched his neck and found a glob of icing resting behind his ear, and I leaped out of bed when I saw him going for my face again, trying to smear it on my cheek.

"You're a disaster," I said. "Come on, help me get the bedding."

We pulled on shorts and tank tops, then I started taking pillow cases off while Michael pulled up the corners of our sheets and folded the bedding into one huge bundle. He wrapped his arms around the load and set off down the hall before I'd finished taking the second pillow case off, startling a sleeping Holly who was sprawled on the floor outside our bedroom doorway. She sprang to her feet and ran after him, tail wagging with excitement. I smiled after them, and a few moments later I followed him with the pillow cases. He already had the washer going when I got to the laundry room on the other side of our kitchen. As I added the pillow cases, he gave me a quick kiss and said, "I'm going to get your gift." He darted away and I heard him thudding up the stairs a moment later. Of course he'd hidden my gift in his office. His favorite room, his safe place. It had been safe to me too, once, but I hadn't been in it since that night.

I walked slowly from the laundry room through the kitchen, still smiling when I thought of his childish excitement about a holiday like Valentine's Day.

I'm not sure what told me something was wrong first.

It must have been a sound, though I don't remember a sound; I remember freezing when I stepped into the living room and my eyes landed on the staircase. There must have been a thud, or maybe a sharp intake of air so quiet it only reached my subconscious, or a gasp, or a whimper from Holly. Something made me expect the crash before it came, and when Michael came down the stairs in a horrible tumble, in the back of my mind I wasn't surprised. I sprang into action and before I knew what I was doing, I was on my knees on the floor beside him, Holly's frantic barking and Michael's groaning like some distant calamity that was happening in someone else's home.

For a moment, I thought he must be dead, seeing the grotesque red that stained his clothes and face. I cradled his face and ran my hands over his chest and arms to assure myself he was alive, he was breathing, he was whole, and I remembered the red was only frosting. I didn't see any real blood and between soft, plaintive moans of his name, asking him if he was okay, begging for him to open his eyes, I whispered to myself that he must be okay. Holly had come down the stairs after him, as soon as she calmed enough to stop barking wildly, and now she hovered over him and began licking his face and whining. His eyes fluttered open and immediately scrunched back closed in a pained grimace.

"Holy shit," he mumbled. I glanced down and noted his ankle twisted in a horrible direction, but he seemed otherwise unhurt on the surface.

"Are you okay? I think your ankle is twisted. Do you feel pain anywhere else?" I asked.

"Everywhere. I don't know. My head, my leg. My back." He stretched out his non-twisted leg and moved his arms around gingerly, then put his palms on the floor and pushed himself up almost to a seated position so he could look at his ankle. "Shit," he said.

"Michael, lie back down. Don't move. I'll call an ambulance."

"No, Jana, no. It's okay."

"Michael, you were unconscious for a second, and we don't know what all you hurt. You need help."

"I know," he said. "I'm not saying I don't, but I don't think I have any broken bones or anything. We can drive to the hospital. With how long an ambulance would take to get here, we'll probably get there faster ourselves anyway."

"Fine, but how are you going to get out to the car?"

"Don't we still have the crutches from the time you twisted your ankle?"

"They're out in the workshop." I said it like a counterargument, like that made them not an option, and he stared at me in pointed irritation, expecting me to jump up and go get them. "I don't want to leave you here," I explained.

"I'm fine. Just go quickly."

I hesitated, and he narrowed his eyes. I didn't know what to say. I didn't want to leave him, but couldn't tell him I was afraid that if I left him alone something even more horrible might happen to him.

"I don't know for sure they're even out there," I lied. "I think I donated them. I can help you. Come on."

He didn't argue further, probably in too much pain to do it, and he allowed me to help him up and drape his arm around my shoulders. He wasn't significantly taller than me, but still held at least fifty pounds over me, and I had to put enormous effort into pretending I wasn't struggling to stay upright under the weight. Somehow, with Holly whining and dancing around us all the way, we reached my car and I got him into the passenger seat. I had to run back in for my purse and keys, and even that seemed risky—a risk to leave him and another risk to enter that house alone, but necessary risks, both. I ran up the path to the front door and leaned into the entryway, calling Holly to follow me. My purse was hanging right inside the door, thankfully, and I snatched it, closed Holly inside, locked the door, and ran back to the car. Michael sat in the passenger seat with his head leaned back and pressed against the headrest, taking deep breaths as he tried to control the pain.

"Did you really donate the crutches?" he asked through tightly clenched teeth as I pulled out of our driveway.

"I'm not sure. I remember thinking about it, and I don't remember seeing them recently." That was a bald lie. I had seen them the last time I was out there and remembered thinking I should find a better storage place for them. "I didn't want to waste time looking," I added.

He nodded shortly and turned to stare out the window in silence, continuing his deep, controlled breaths.

I squeezed his hand briefly. I didn't like lying, but couldn't bring myself to tell him that at some point, somewhere between my terror at thinking he might be dead and my relief at seeing him open his eyes, I had seen something else, something like a shadow, a figure, standing at the top of the stairs where he fell.

Chapter Twenty-Four

I **DIDN'T WANT** to come home. The bright lights of the hospital, the constant background hum of voices and footsteps and beeping, people appearing and disappearing with smiles and banal comments. Bemused expressions at our frosting streaks and the cupcake in our hair. Teasing about seeing other Valentine's Day mornings that got wilder than intended, teasing that made me flush while Michael laughed. But several hours and tests, scans, and monitoring instructions for a mild concussion later, we pulled back into our driveway and faced our house again.

I had asked what made him fall. I was afraid to ask, didn't do it until we were at the hospital, safe in our enclosure of strangers and public space.

"I don't know," he said. "I remember bending down to pet Holly as I was taking the first step down the stairs, and I guess I lost my balance." It was then that his mouth fell slightly open with a sharp intake of air and his eyes met mine with sudden realization. "Your gift! Did you see it?"

"No. I don't remember seeing it at all. Were you holding it?"

"Yeah. I must've dropped it."

"Will it be broken?" I asked, prying now for clues about my gift. Back to normal life. Jana and Michael, Michael and Jana, pretending to be normal and ignoring the shadow that lurked in our home.

"Maybe," he said with a smile. "Or maybe it'll have run off. Or melted. There's no telling."

"How mysterious," I said.

I wondered if it would still be there, waiting on the steps. If it wasn't, would he finally see? Maybe he would admit then that it wasn't lost balance that had made him fall, it wasn't dreams that explained my nighttime visitations, it wasn't the wind that ruined my table, it wasn't sleep deprivation making me hallucinate, it wasn't the million other rationales our minds supply when things don't make sense.

More likely, he'd say the dog must have eaten it. He'd drop to his knees and smother her in kisses while asking her, *"Did you eat Jana's gift? Did you do that? Did you? Where did you put it?"* Then he'd forget all about it, or pretend he did.

I got out of the car first and pulled the new hospital crutches out of the backseat, then circled around to the passenger side to help Michael out of the car. He was able to manage on his own once he got his crutches situated, and we began moving slowly up the path to the front door.

Whatever's waiting for us, we'll face it together, I guess.

I almost wanted there to be something. But of course there wouldn't be. It was all mine, my torment, threatening everything important to me while those things continued existing in bland complacence.

The envelope was the first thing I saw, looking past the flurry that was Holly and ignoring the coos and exclamations that were Michael, I saw the envelope laying neatly on the top step and my eyes fixated on it.

Trick? Or treat?

"You found your gift." Michael followed my gaze to the envelope.

Treat.

I started up the stairs, pretending to be excited, hoping I looked it, wondering what Michael would do, could do, if something was waiting for me at the top. I got three-quarters of the way up the stairs and leaned over, snatching the envelope and hurrying back down where Michael waited for me, his eyes following me while he managed to lean on his crutches in a way that made him look nonchalant and relaxed.

"Let me guess," I said, holding up the envelope, "Cupcake gift certificate?"

I pulled out a voucher for a massage package. If I'd been given three chances to guess what Michael had gotten me for Valentine's Day, I think I'd have gotten it right with chances to spare, and I loved him for that. I said thank you and kissed him, not having to stretch since he was hunched over on his crutches, careful not to lean on him. "I stashed your gift in the workshop. I'll grab it in a bit." I wanted to wait until he was settled so he wouldn't hobble out there with me and see the crutches.

At the same time, a splash of color in the kitchen that didn't belong, that wasn't there when we left, grabbed my attention.

I took a cautious step toward the kitchen, forgetting Michael's gift in the workshop and the telltale crutches keeping it company, and saw it was flowers, bright orange and wild and bursting from a vase they had already outgrown, stark against the cream-colored walls, off-white cabinets, and dark brown marble countertops.

"Those are nice." Michael's voice in my ear behind me made me jump. "Where did they come from?" He had shifted from the front door and was peering over my shoulder into the kitchen.

Why the fuck does he always sound so unconcerned?

I approached the counter slowly, trying not to wonder again what Michael could do if there was something other than flowers there. When I reached the counter, I noticed the small box of truffles tucked behind the flowers. They were Michael's favorite. I picked up a small note that was stuck to the counter in front of the flowers.

Sorry your Valentine's Day got cut short! With a little heart and a signature in the corner.

"It's from Ivy," I called over my shoulder, but I wasn't as relieved as I should have been. Ivy had come into the house, alone, without warning, and it occurred to me in that moment that I hadn't heard from her in hours; that other than exchanging a few messages when I arrived at the hospital and her sending Michael a sympathetic message shortly after, I hadn't talked to her, hadn't heard from her; she hadn't checked in or asked what was happening or when we would be arriving home.

The still silence of the house pressed in on me and I struggled to find my breath. I saw her in my mind, using her spare key without a thought and walking loudly through the entryway—she probably wouldn't even glance up the stairs or down the dark hall, Ivy wouldn't worry about such things, couldn't be bothered by silly fears—she'd greet Holly cheerfully and kiss her right on the nose without caring that Holly's return kiss would involve a tongue up her nose. I never understood how she and Michael could not care about something like that, could accept dog drool in their nostrils without minding, and I wondered if it meant they were kinder people than me. And then she would have walked into the kitchen, probably not even flipping on lights as she went. *"My biggest fear is myself,"* she'd once told me. And she would set the flowers and chocolates on the counter, scribble out her note, and arrange it all to catch our attention and surprise us.

In my mind's eye, I watched her from the stairway, saw the nape of her neck bent over her note, her curls tied together on top of her head, saw her stick the pen in her mouth as she pressed the sticky note onto the countertop, then watched from the living room, a little closer, then from the kitchen doorway, closer now, close enough now to see the tiny rose tattoo peeking from behind her ear, to see the miniscule thorns on the stem.

"Aww, this is so nice of her. She didn't have to . . . Jana? Jana, what's wrong?"

Michael's voice called out while I crumpled to the floor, falling, seeing spots and gasping for breath. "She was here," I gasped. "She was here and now I haven't heard from her in hours."

"That doesn't mean anything." His voice sounded desperate and confused and suddenly I realized he was kneeling on the floor beside me, his crutches in a heap beside him.

"Michael . . . Your ankle. You shouldn't be on the floor."

"You fell. What was I supposed to do?"

"Ivy . . . " I didn't know how much to say or how to say it. *There might be something in our house and she was here alone.* "I'm afraid something happened. I just have a feeling."

"Okay. We'll call her, okay? Give me your phone." He pulled my phone out of my hand and called Ivy from my history; she was never more than the third line down.

She picked up after the first ring and Michael held the phone between us so her voice came clearly to both of us. "Hi! Did y'all get home yet? How's Michael feeling? Do you need anything?"

Michael and my eyes met over the phone, and he smiled at her rapid-fire questioning.

"We're good," I said, trying to focus on the relief I felt and not the embarrassment at having caused yet another scene. "Thank you so much for the flowers and chocolates. You're amazing."

"I am! But no for real, I just felt awful about your first Valentine's Day after getting married going so bad. Hope the rest of your day turns out okay—what's left of it anyway, damn. Y'all really just got home? What'd they do there, heart transplant?"

"You would think," Michael joined in. "Anyway, thanks Ivy.

Jana is really going to enjoy these chocolates. I might get one or two, but thanks for thinking of her."

"Very funny," I said.

"Right," Ivy laughed. "We'll pretend they're for Jana."

We said our goodbyes and I helped Michael to his feet. Ivy was safe and our home was exactly as we left it. The doubt I could never fully banish returned, leaving me wondering yet again if it was all me, if it was all my own mind. I touched the delicate flower petals lightly, and turned to leave the kitchen. I had forgotten that Michael would expect an explanation, and I forgot it until I took a step toward the living room and realized Michael stayed still, raising his eyebrows at me and standing there like a broken statue instead of moving to the couch to rest.

"I can't explain it," I said shortly. I knew it wasn't good enough, I knew it wasn't fair, but I was so tired.

"Try." There was no room for argument in his voice.

"I thought I saw something up there," I answered, weary and cross. "When you fell. It wasn't clear. It looked like a dark figure. Just a blink and then it was gone." Michael opened his mouth to respond and I cut him off. "I know—I imagined it."

"If you knew you imagined it, why would you get so upset about Ivy being alone here? Why would that scare you so much?"

"I had a 'what if it was real' moment. I hadn't heard from her in hours and I was afraid."

His eyes held mine for a moment longer before the pain he was holding back finally flickered through them and he relented with a wince, giving up, moving slowly toward the living room. "Well, I am sorry about our Valentine's Day getting ruined," he said. "I guess we'll have to spend the rest of the day stuffing our faces with cupcakes, candy, and pizza while we watch bad movies." His voice had risen into false complaining, pretending he was dreading an afternoon spent that way, and I followed him with a smile.

"I'm sure you had something much more sophisticated planned for us," I said.

"Oh, yes. But now you'll never know. I can't go telling you my ideas; maybe I'll save it for next year."

We settled on the couch together, Michael raising his foot to rest it on the coffee table after I arranged a cushion for him. It was only then that I could begin to think objectively and question the abject terror that had seized me at the idea of Ivy being alone in my home. It was true that I no longer had any comfort or peace when I was left in a room by myself, that I sought Michael's constant presence as naturally as I could, that I would not relish coming home from work to an empty house again. Yet there was a sense of the familiar in all those scenes, and the dread was a wretched, slow, sinking dread, while I watched in helpless misery as it became my normal state of being. The idea of Ivy becoming somehow touched by this unknown thing, getting hurt or being infected by the darkness that had invaded my home, made me sick, made it all more than I could set aside and smile over.

If I had a monster, it was supposed to be my own.

Chapter Twenty-Five

IT WAS HARD going back to work. I was afraid of leaving Michael alone, not knowing if whatever haunted me remained behind when I left or how far it could go. If it wanted him out of the way. But he was so certain nothing had caused his fall but himself, that nothing so much as brushed against him. So I dressed for work and planned to leave him alone, though I lingered in the doorway to his office and watched him a moment before I left for the day, settled at his desk with his coffee, water, and snacks, crutches leaned against the wall beside him, Holly warming his free foot and avoiding the hurt one.

"Are you sure you don't need anything else?" I asked.

"Go to work," he said. "You've piled more granola bars here than I can eat in a week. It's a sprained ankle. You know I can still walk, right? I'm surprised you didn't insist on a catheter."

"It's not too late."

"Ha. Out. Go to work."

"Fine. I love you."

"Love you, too."

And so I worked, though I couldn't keep myself from messaging Michael nearly hourly to check in, messages he answered with patient humor. Otherwise, I moved through my day as I had before everything started, as if things were the same, though everywhere I looked now, I wondered; wondered what else I didn't understand and if it was everywhere. Wondered if anyone else had dreams that were not really dreams.

Sometimes I thought people were looking at me differently at work. That they noticed the cracks, knew how tired I was, caught the fear in my eyes. But in that one area of my life, at least, I clung to my normalcy. I met deadlines, I maintained the same high level of accuracy I always had, I responded to emails in less than a day, I returned client calls promptly. I listened to my voice on phone calls and at meetings, calm and professional, and I marveled at myself.

Maybe I was quieter. Maybe I wasn't seeking out new projects with as much enthusiasm as when I started. Maybe I stopped paying as much attention to my team. I didn't say anything when Lex started coming in late every morning, and I passed the three new clients from Julieta to two people beneath me without a thought. I hadn't been asked to do any presentations lately and a few times I walked by a large conference room with glass walls and saw Julieta or Devin or even Maria talking to people I didn't know. I wondered if I was deemed too incompetent for presentations now—but then I knew I was being ridiculous, that Julieta and Devin and Maria all regularly had client meetings in our offices, as I did.

Whatever the reason, I dreaded what was coming when Devin called an impromptu staff meeting late on a Friday afternoon. I sent a quick message to Michael before Devin launched into his spiel: *Still doing ok?* I asked.

"Don't worry, it isn't bad news," Devin said as we gathered, flashing his charming smile to the group.

We're gathered here today to discuss a growing problem on our team...

"As most of you know," he said, "we've been exploring ways to restructure our teams so the client work load is distributed a little more evenly. Certain service areas have grown so much more rapidly than we expected . . . "

This is an intervention. Let's go around the circle and talk about what bothers us most about the way Jana's been acting lately.

"...With Julieta's team handling a lot of the newest services, expertise in those areas is becoming very focused, and I know a lot of people have expressed interest in learning more . . . "

For me, personally, it's the makeup. And the hair. The makeup and the hair. One minute she looks clean and attractive every day, and now she's frizzy and plain. It's distracting for everyone.

By the end of the meeting, Julieta's team was two people bigger—I tried to tell myself that didn't mean anything, wasn't relevant to me—while nothing had changed on my team. I could tell as Devin spoke that several people were already aware of what was going to be said, already in the know about the changes that were coming, while I stood clueless on the sidelines.

There was a time when I would have been annoyed that I hadn't been part of those discussions. I was a manager in the department, after all. I would have been insecure and worried about Julieta's team growing while mine stayed the same and no one considered adding new services or new people under me. That day, I was relieved not to be involved in any of it. All I could think of was getting back to my office to see if Michael had answered my message yet. I darted away from the gathering the moment Devin finished speaking, not meeting his eyes, chiding myself when I was halfway back to my office for not at least putting on a polite front and congratulating Julieta for her successes.

Michael had answered my text before the meeting ended: *I'm still alive, weirdo.*

And I tried to let it go, to stop hovering over Michael every moment when I got home. To not live in fear that he would be taken from me. The shadow was only a shadow, the easiest of all my dreams and nightmares to explain away. The accident could have been just that.

Chapter Twenty-Six

T HE STEAMING WATER pelted my skin while I scrubbed, creating a blanket of suds, and my head slowly cleared of the morning fog. The sleeping pills Dr. Goulding prescribed left me groggy, but rested, and I was thankful for the blank, dreamless nights.

The gratitude was fleeting.

I ran the cloth up and down my arms, down one leg and back up, then down the other. I paused as I came back up, when the cloth reached my inner left thigh. Bent over in the small shower stall, I noticed a mark I hadn't seen before. Small, red indentations in the tender skin of my thigh, like a row of teeth. It hadn't been there the night before, and even if I had somehow missed it, Michael hadn't even come close to biting me there the last time we'd been together.

I bent and looked closer, and it was unmistakable.

I dropped the cloth. I wanted to scream. I had just enough forethought to move my shaking hand to the shower nozzle and tilt it to face the wall so that when I collapsed onto the floor, the water wouldn't hit my face. And I collapsed. A sob rose in my throat instead of a scream, a sob that stretched across my chest, so strong it hurt to breathe, and it came out strangled and ugly like a trapped animal.

It hadn't left. Of course it hadn't left. I had been naive enough to hope that because I didn't remember it, it wasn't there while I slept. But it waited until I fell asleep, a vulnerable and drug-soaked sleep, and . . . then what? I wanted to throw up, wondering what had happened, how, why—with Michael right next to me? I sat on the tile floor in the steam-filled shower with my face on my knees. My body felt like a thing not my own, a violated, separate, senseless thing I could not protect.

I don't know how many moments passed in that broken panic,

THE FACE YOU WEAR

but eventually I started wondering what I was supposed to do. I wracked my brain thinking of all the things women are told to do in situations when we don't know what's happened to us.

I told myself the bite had to be the only thing that had happened. Michael had been sleeping beside me every night and he wasn't such a deep sleeper that someone could have come in and . . . the word hovered in a part of my mind I didn't want to look at.

Have I been raped?

No.

Even with the pills, I had to believe I would have woken up if anything else happened. Or Michael would have.

The thought of anything happening to me with Michael sleeping soundly next to me made me nauseous.

None of it made sense.

It hadn't left.

I sat there wondering what to do, running through the options in my mind yet again.

Now that I'd been hurt, maybe Michael would take me seriously. He wouldn't laugh at that. I imagined wrapping my towel around myself and returning to our bedroom where he still slept and shaking him awake. Allowing myself to be held while I cried into his chest and told him and showed him what had happened to me. His eyes would flash with that rare anger, so very rare for Michael, and he would demand to be allowed to fix it. And he would ask me questions.

When did it happen?

Did you take your pill last night?

Are you sure it wasn't there before?

How did you sleep through that?

How could it have happened with me in the room?

Then we'd watch the security cameras. We'd watch the cameras and try to figure out how someone came into our home without the cameras showing and then there would be police and the same questions again and the same review of the cameras and finally shrugging and Michael's anger would fade and he'd look worried instead, and he'd still hold me and comfort me and promise to figure everything out but the question would be in his eyes and the doubt would be mixed in with the worry.

What do you think happened, Jana?

What do you think you saw?
What do you think that mark is?
Could it be a rash, maybe?
How do you think it happened?
It wasn't enough. Sitting there on the tile floor as the water turned lukewarm instead of hot, I couldn't think of anything to do, any way to explain what was happening that wouldn't get me a diagnosis that came with a lifelong prescription and monitoring. And so, like so many things I couldn't control, I set it aside. I would continue my sessions with Dr. Goulding, but I would stop taking the sleeping pills. I would find a way to show Michael or Ivy what was happening. I wasn't sure which of them would be easier to convince, but I would get one of them on my side, and then the other.

Chapter Twenty-Seven

AN IDEA CAME to me later that day. If I'd had the idea a few weeks ago, before the thing in the office and before resuming my sessions with Dr. Goulding, I might have tried to hide it from Michael; I might have tried to do it without telling him. I might have even wanted to try and catch him unaware, to see if he had anything of his own to hide. But now, I was resolved to talk to him about it first. To do it the right way. I was done suspecting him.

No more hiding, lying, sweeping dark things into dark corners. Other than the bite mark.

I had taken a picture of the mark close up on my cell phone, and it looked almost innocuous out of context. A small red circle, probably not even noticeable if it wasn't pointed out.

But for me it throbbed in my brain and pressed against the back of my eyelids.

I didn't say anything to Dr. Goulding about it. I had told her about the shadow on the stairs, but she acted like it was so normal, so expected, even mundane, to imagine such a thing.

"I see shadows all the time, Jana, everyone does; I wouldn't even classify that as a waking nightmare."

Seeing how nonchalant she was about it, I couldn't bring myself to tell her anything else. Besides, I finally had the beginnings of a plan. A weak one, but it was a beginning. And I needed to sell it.

Michael and I had been getting along wonderfully lately, as I told Dr. Goulding again that morning. I didn't want to disturb our tranquility. I needed to frame what I wanted the right way, in a way that Michael would accept without those raised eyebrows, those questioning eyes filled with concern. I needed him to not only accept it, but to think it was a good idea.

We were having spaghetti for dinner that night. Michael made the sauce from scratch and the house was permeated with scents of garlic and parmesan. I could smell it all the way from our bedroom when I went to change clothes. Slacks, blouse, and loafers were replaced with jeans, a t-shirt, and socks. We were eating inside that evening, because even though the covered porch would shelter us from the solid sheet of rain enclosing the house, it couldn't protect us from the sharp chill that bit through the old uninsulated wood and flowed openly through the screened sections. We had reached that point of winter that comes each year, where I began to tire of the oppressive, dreary weather, when the snow means mud instead of sleighing and the cold means frozen cars and dangerous roads instead of long-missed boots and soft scarves.

I sipped my wine slowly as we began to eat.

"Should you be drinking wine with the sleeping pills Dr. Goulding gave you?" Michael had asked me when he saw me reaching for a wine glass.

"I was going to skip taking them tonight," I answered. *And tomorrow. And forever.* "They make me groggy. I'll let Dr. Goulding know and see if she recommends something different."

It wasn't a lie if I really planned to tell her, I reasoned. *I forgot today, but that doesn't mean I don't plan to tell her.*

I watched him covertly as he digested my response, but he didn't seem upset or concerned. Still, I decided to let at least a few other topics act as a buffer before I brought up my main idea. It was a bad combination, I realized. Making him believe I was dropping pills because I don't need them while telling him I needed something else.

"What do you want for your birthday?" he asked.

"It's over a month away," I said.

"Fine, be that way." He made a childish face at me. "I already knew what I was getting you anyway."

"Is that so?"

"Yup. Just had to make double sure you didn't have some special request you've been sitting on."

"Nothing comes to mind," I said. A few moments rolled by in silence as we ate.

"This is delicious," I said. "Thank you for making it."

"Sure thing."

A few more moments passed. I wondered if it was the right time to bring it up or if I should let some more conversation go by first. But Michael was wholly focused on his food, not seeming to notice or mind the silence, and I had to remind myself that normally I don't either. We had never had a problem sitting in silence together.

"What's on your mind?" he asked, drawing my attention from the gray, misty windows where I was watching the steady rain continuing to drop.

"I was thinking that it might be a good idea to put a camera in our bedroom to monitor my sleep." There. I said it.

He let out a short, dubious laugh that didn't bode well for my mission. "No, thank you," he said. "I don't need my snoring recorded any more than it already is." He gave me a meaningful, accusatory look. I had recorded his snoring once, early in our relationship, and I played the sound back in his ear so he woke with a start, looking around wildly to determine the source of the sound while I giggled uncontrollably.

I gave him a slight smile at the memory, knowing he was being playful, but pressed doggedly on. "For one, having a camera would give me an easy way to figure out which interactions are dreams and which aren't, so I don't have to keep asking you."

"I don't mind you asking me," he said, as he filled his mouth with another bite of spaghetti.

"For two," I continued as if I hadn't heard him, "it might be helpful to see if I'm doing anything abnormal in my sleep. If I talk, sit up, sleepwalk, toss and turn more than usual, anything like that. It'd be good to know."

He took another bite without saying anything this time.

"Three—I know we more or less ruled out the idea of someone doing this to us, since I saw the thing in the office and that clearly wasn't . . . you know." I shifted uncomfortably.

"Real?"

"Sure." I ground my teeth. "But having that extra layer of security would still make me feel better. With all the weird things that happened, knowing once and for all that there wasn't anyone doing anything to me would be nice."

He set down his fork and brought his hand to his chin, scratching it thoughtfully with his elbow resting on the table. "Did you talk to Dr. Goulding about this?"

"I will. She mentioned that it's something some of her other clients with sleep problems have done." I tried to remember if she had said that, exactly. I was pretty sure she had mentioned something like it.

"All right, if it'll make you feel better," he said. "We're putting it on your side of the room though."

"Of course, that's what I want."

"Do you want to go get the equipment sometime this weekend?"

"That would be great." I smiled and reached for the bottle of wine, relieved that the conversation was over and that I had successfully made my case.

***

The weekend didn't come in time. That night was the first night in weeks that I went to bed without the strong sleeping pills Dr. Goulding prescribed me, but I was groggy under the heavy cloud of too much wine.

"Are you feeling okay?" Michael asked.

I was lying on my side facing the door, and he perched on the edge of the bed in front of me. I blinked the sleep from my eyes and tried to focus on him, a dim figure in the darkness. I wasn't sure how long I had been asleep, and tried to remember if I had even said goodnight to him before passing out.

We had stayed in the dining room for nearly an hour after we finished eating. I had continued drinking wine and Michael sipped his slowly; I remembered opening a second bottle at some point in the evening, but I wasn't sure how much of the first bottle I was responsible for. We sat together in the living room after that, watching a show and drinking.

I struggled to orient myself in the blackness of our bedroom, my head still swimming.

"Jana? Are you okay?" he repeated.

"I'm fine. Just tired," I said.

"You've seemed distracted lately," he said. Sympathetic, not judgmental. "A little distant. Weren't you sleeping better with the sleeping pills?"

"Maybe. But it isn't good sleep," I said, starting to feel annoyed that he was waking me up to talk about this again. "I'll tell Dr. Goulding I stopped and make sure it's okay."

"Have you been having nightmares when you take them?" His voice was soft and soothing.

"No," I admitted. "But I don't usually have nightmares when you come to bed with me either." I wasn't sure anymore if that was true, but I still preferred it.

"You sleep better when you don't go to bed alone?" he asked, his question laced with understanding and affection. He dragged his finger over my cheek softly as he spoke.

"I think so," I said.

"You think that helps?"

"Yes."

"So, you think you can sleep without me?" With this question, his tone shifted from concern to detached curiosity, from loving and sincere to mocking, and the words hung like a threat between us.

You think you can sleep without me? Not a question, not a question at all. A challenge.

My head swam. *I shouldn't have drunk so much.*

I stared through the darkness at the figure sitting next to me on the bed, not knowing what to say.

"What?" I asked, my heart speeding up.

"Do you think you can sleep without me?" When he repeated it, his voice dropped back into an innocent question again. Genuine and concerned. Just checking in. Maybe making the implicit offer to come to bed with me if I was afraid. Yet I suddenly did not want him to.

"Oh. Yes, I think I can sleep okay alone," I said.

"Do you?"

In that moment, the bed shifted behind me and ever so slowly, as though my brain was stalling, frozen, unable to comprehend what it sensed, I began to realize there was a heavy weight lying in bed behind me. I arched my back ever so slightly, a fraction of an inch, moving imperceptibly away from the figure sitting in front of me, and my hip was met with a body, solid and unmistakable, behind me.

The moment I felt him there, I heard the sound of Michael breathing, deep asleep, dead to the world, dead to anything happening around him. My breath became trapped in my chest.

I must still be dreaming. My eyes began to fill with tears even as I assured myself it wasn't real.

He knows it. He knows I've realized it and he isn't saying a word because he likes it, he likes this. The air trembled with his amusement, so thick I could feel it.

I wanted to reach for the light on the bedside table, but he was right there, almost blocking me. I stayed frozen on my side, not daring to move or reach out.

Why does he still sit here?

I couldn't know which was real: the heavy, invisible weight behind me or the dark figure before my eyes. I felt a sense of revulsion toward the man or thing sitting on the edge of my bed—yet was terrified that it was Michael after all, and that at any moment he would stand up and walk out of the room, leaving me with whatever was behind me.

But it has to be Michael behind me.

The gentle snore and the warmth radiating from him convinced me, and set me against the Michael sitting on the edge of my bed.

He is going to get up and walk out of this room, then I will turn on the light and see that Michael is sleeping beside me and everything is okay. Or if I am only dreaming it's here, I will wake up. Then I will turn on the light and see that Michael is sleeping beside me and everything is okay. I will wake up. Wake up.

But it sat there. So close, almost touching me, perfectly at ease. Perfectly silent. I couldn't tell in the darkness if he was looking at me. Staring at me. Watching my frozen panic.

Slowly, I began to reach toward the light on the other side of him.

He didn't move. A shadow in the darkness.

My hand crept toward my nightstand, skirting him with as wide a berth as I could give. Still he said nothing.

Strain filled me from my stomach to my throat as I inched tortuously closer to the light. My armpits were damp and sweat began to gather on my forehead. The pressure made me want to scream and finally I couldn't stand moving slowly anymore, couldn't stand another second in the darkness with him. My hand was halfway toward the nightstand when I straightened my arm in a burst of movement and pressed the switch on my lamp.

There was nothing.

Michael was asleep and our room was empty.

I piled my pillows behind me so I could sit in the bed propped up and stare out at the room around me. I was thankful that our platform bedframe meant there was no space under the bed to check, but my eyes searched the rest of the room, pausing on any space that seemed capable of hiding something. But there was nothing. I turned my attention to Michael, still asleep, his face shaded by my pillow so the lamp on my nightstand didn't shine on his face. I reached out quietly and touched my index finger to his face, warm and vibrating with his soft snores, his deep breaths.

I shifted my legs from under the covers and scanned them in the yellow light. There were no new marks. I didn't intend to fall back asleep. I left the light on all night and stayed propped up against my pillows, watching the room and the door.

At some point, I did fall asleep.

I woke with a piercing headache that made me curse the version of myself who was foolish enough to think wine was delicious, or that alcohol could help me sleep. I always knew better in the morning. And in the light of day, with Michael still sleeping innocently beside me and no evidence of any intrusion in our bedroom or our home, the tiny part of me that still clung to a rational answer for all of it could explain the events of the night before as hazy, alcohol-infused nightmares.

Chapter Twenty-Eight

I **WAS DETERMINED** not to sleep another night without the cameras. Michael was still healing, and I knew it was unlikely that he would want to go with me to the store any time soon, so I decided to pick them up myself after work. But when I messaged him to let him know my plans and that I'd be late home, he answered, "I already ordered them."

"What do you mean?" I asked.

"Just had to add cameras to our security package, silly. All taken care of." He added a heart at the end of his message, and I wanted to scream.

"When will they get here?" I texted back. I tried to swallow my panic that I wouldn't have them that day, that I had to sleep another night in that room without any way to prove what was happening.

"Tomorrow."

Tomorrow was too far.

I messaged Ivy next, praying she would be free to meet after work. She responded with enthusiastic assent almost immediately, and I messaged Michael again to let him know I was going to see Ivy and would still be home late. I couldn't say why I needed to see her, and I wasn't sure what I would have the courage to tell her; I only knew I didn't want to go home. I knew I couldn't stay away all night, but I could delay the inevitable by a couple of hours.

We met at a cafe near her bookshop that served everything from pastries and coffee to fondue and local beer.

I ordered a martini and hesitated, looking at Ivy. "Are you sure . . . "

She nodded dismissively and waved her assent. I finished my order, but couldn't keep my eyes from landing on the tiny infinity sobriety tattoo nestled between her thumb and forefinger. She pretended not to notice me looking.

"Aren't you going to regret having it in a place where everyone can see?" I had asked her shortly after she first got it, years ago.

"No. That's kinda the point," she'd said. "I can't hide from it. I don't wanna hide from it."

"That's great. Anything that helps." I wanted to be supportive. "I don't think I could handle having strangers know something so personal about my past."

She smiled knowingly. "No, I don't imagine you could." There was a soft understanding in her voice, with no judgment. "But I don't mind it."

She was an open book. The first time Michael met her, he teased me afterward that he'd learned more about me from one evening with my sister than he had in the three months we'd been dating at the time.

She watched me take my first drink and I tried not to look overeager.

"What is it? Are the dreams still bad?" she asked.

I wanted to tell her everything. I imagined motioning her over to my side of the booth and scooting into the corner so the light didn't shine on me, then lifting my skirt enough to show her the mark. I had reached for slacks when I dressed that morning, but then grabbed a skirt instead without acknowledging why. I wondered what she would do if I was brave enough to show her; if she would get upset and demand I leave my house and stay with her. Part of me wanted that, too, though my rational self didn't think it'd help.

And maybe she'd react differently. Maybe she'd squint and stare at the mark without recognition, and I would have to tell her it was a bite mark that appeared in my sleep. Then she'd give me that worried, sympathetic look and reply that it looked more like a rash or a scratch than a bite.

"Yes, the dreams are still bad," I said instead, unmoving.

I sounded tired. I'd told her about the thing in the office, but it was after I had already met with Dr. Goulding and decided to play along with the waking nightmare theory. It was a decision I was beginning to regret. I'd been so afraid of Ivy thinking I was turning into our mother, of Michael losing faith in me; but if I had held my ground and tried harder to make them see, would they have? I would make them believe me eventually, but not until I had a better explanation and something to prove it, at least a little. Not until I sounded less like our mother.

"What is it now?" she asked.

I didn't feel like telling her Creepy Michael stories of a man that sat on the edge of my bed while my husband slept next to me. "It's all a bit blurry," I said.

"You look exhausted." Her eyebrows were pressed together in concern, and she bit her lip as she stared at me, waiting. Waiting for me to share more or to tell her it was okay. I couldn't do either. She waited another moment for me to say something.

"Jana, what do you need? What can I do?"

"I don't know."

"What does Dr. Goulding say?"

"She tells me to take sleeping pills, but I don't like taking something so strong." I knew Ivy would understand that. "And I haven't met with her since the latest dream."

"It wasn't another one like the Michael monster in his office, was it?"

"No." Just hearing her talking about it made my heart pound, and sweat began to form under my arms. "Not like that. It was nothing major."

She reached across the table and squeezed the hand that wasn't wrapped around the martini. "Jana, you know you can tell me anything, right? I'm not going to judge you. I only want to help."

"I know that. I wish I knew what to ask you for." I forced a smile and she put her hand back in her lap. "Besides, you have your own stuff. Speaking of, do you have more pictures of the place you want?"

I spent the next hour listening to Ivy's updates about moving, the bookshop, another relationship she'd decided to end before it started because he was intense and she had no interest in being tied down. It was a pleasant distraction for a while, but it was too hard pretending with Ivy that things were okay. As much as I had no interest in going home, knowing there was nothing to keep it away, I knew I had to go sooner or later.

I had fleeting thoughts of wild excuses to spend the night at Ivy's—I thought of making up an early morning work meeting (but her apartment was only twenty minutes closer to my office than our home, and I had no extra work clothes with me). I was tempted to drink too heavily and make myself unable to drive home, but Ivy would probably think nothing of driving me home and I couldn't trust my drunk self to navigate that mess.

Besides, I didn't know what would happen if I stayed away. I pictured Michael hurtling to the floor from the top of the stairs again, and shuddered.

And then the bite mark. Like a horrible "hello" to let me know it was still there, that even if I slept in drugged peace and didn't know what was happening around me, that didn't mean nothing was happening.

Chapter Twenty-Nine

I WILL NOT SLEEP.

The pillows were bunched behind me and I sat up in bed, knees drawn toward my chest, with a book I hadn't been reading resting against my thighs. It was already after one in the morning and Michael was sound asleep.

I'd had coffee after dinner while Michael was upstairs; I dropped ice cubes in it and gulped it down so he wouldn't catch me drinking it and ask me why, and I lit a candle in the kitchen to mask the smell. Afterwards I checked on him, pretending I just wanted to say hi, and confirmed he was planning on staying upstairs for another hour or so. Then I rushed downstairs and repeated the process twice more.

I'd have laughed at myself if the fear didn't make me want to throw up instead.

I tried to remember the last time I had stayed up all night. There were plenty of times when I was a child, before Ivy was old enough to manage our finances and do the grocery shopping for us, that a rumbling stomach kept us up until the sun rose and we could try again to find a way to feed ourselves.

There were a couple of times in college. Part of me wished there had been more; my all-nighters weren't for any exciting reasons, but only happened when finals week had me scrambling to study and finish semester projects. I'd been so reserved in college, so intimidated by the loud confidence budding around me, and terrified that if I didn't put every ounce of energy I had into making perfect grades I would end up right back in the trailer with my mom. I used to dream about it all the time. Waking up in my old bed and trying to walk out the front door but somehow finding myself in the kitchen instead, or back in my bedroom, or wandering around the tiny backyard without remembering why I was there.

My eyelids began to droop as my mind wandered and I slapped my cheek lightly.

How hard can it be to stay awake for one night?

But in time, my eyelids began to fall.

***

That night, I had a dream I knew was a dream from the start.

I was in our backyard and the light cast over the outside was a strange yellow-green, the way a late summer afternoon sometimes looks after a storm. I stared toward the forest behind our house, our special patch of wilderness that was one of the main things that drew me to the house in the first place. But I didn't feel affection for it now. I stared toward it because I knew something was there, watching, something that might crawl out at any moment. I didn't know how I knew, but I was standing in the yard expressly to wait for it.

I stood some twenty steps from the tree line, and the trees were trapped behind a haze, almost shimmering in the yellow light. I wondered if I could walk through it if I tried, and as soon as I wondered it, I knew I didn't want to, didn't want at all to take even one step closer.

What's behind me? I wondered, thinking it should be my house but not knowing for sure and inexplicably unable to turn my head to check.

My eyes stayed glued to the trees, roaming left and right along the entire edge, searching.

I froze in position, bare feet sinking slightly into the wet ground.

I was waiting for something.

A shape shifted behind the haze and my eyes focused on it. Through the trees, I could see a dark blur, one moment formless, the next reaching out with long limbs; one moment drifting to the side, the next moment crawling closer. It was growing. The pulsing mass dragged slowly forward and pressed against the film dividing the darkness of the woods from the yellow-lit grass in front of me. Any moment, it was going to pass the fragile barrier into the territory before me, and I couldn't move away from it—couldn't turn and run into the house, couldn't look away, couldn't open my mouth and call out, couldn't even breathe.

It pressed and pressed against the thin film, and I knew it would split apart and I didn't want to see. With great effort, I found

I could move one small part of myself; I could close my eyes, and I did. I squeezed my eyes shut, not wanting to see the shape in the clear light, not wanting to know what would happen if the film tore. And when I opened them, the haze was gone, the wood lit by the same yellow-green light that shone on me, and it was Michael walking toward me with a small smile on his face and his hand held slightly out, posed to take mine. When he reached me and held my hand in his, I could finally move my head, and I pulled my strained eyes from the woods with relief and looked down.

I was wearing the sleeveless cream-colored dress I had worn for our wedding.

CHAPTER THIRTY

I **DIDN'T RELAX** once we had the camera set up in the bedroom. I thought I would, I thought it would give me peace of mind, but at that point I'd already fallen for it too many times. I let myself think it would stop when we put in the security system, or when I drank the dreams away, or when I told Michael about it, or when I started therapy, or when I took sleeping pills; each of these things was supposed to help, supposed to make it stop. It always found a way. I wanted to believe that another camera would be the solution, the thing it couldn't get around, but I didn't believe it. I wouldn't be fooled into false security again.

Every morning, I went to check the recording from the night before and I watched myself sleep with a sick, tense feeling in my stomach. I found myself pausing the video every few minutes, scrutinizing shadows in the room, movements of the comforter, my own body flinching or tossing in my sleep.

I didn't know what I was looking for. Aside from another Michael sauntering into the frame and waving at the camera while my Michael slept blissfully, I couldn't imagine anything happening that would help me make my case. But even if the camera was nothing but a preventive measure, something that kept it away from me while I slept, it was worth it.

And life continued while I waited. Michael healed enough to stop using the crutches, though he limped slightly and enjoyed saying he couldn't do dishes or laundry while he was "infirm". Sometimes he watched the video footage with me for a few moments, quick to point out when it looked like I might be drooling or I stole his pillow or other such offenses.

I pointed out that we had had the camera for several nights and this was the first time I took his pillow and he hushed me with a kiss, pausing the video and taking the tablet from my hands and putting it on the nightstand.

"Oh, hold on, let me turn off the camera," I said, pulling away from him.

"Or don't," he said, his crooked grin mischievous and suggestive.

I laughed and pressed the button. "Probably better to leave some things unseen."

Camera off, candle on, light off. Camera back on before we went to sleep. It became a routine for us. The dreams had been quiet, my sleep had been a little better, and Michael was loving and concerned. He seemed to have finally adjusted his sleep schedule for good, going to bed at the same time as me every night. He even made it seem like it was because he simply wanted to be near me and wanted to be there for me, instead of making me feel like an invalid who needed constant attention because I couldn't handle being alone. And as a result, we were more affectionate than we'd ever been before, except for maybe the first few months after our relationship became serious.

I tried not to hope it would stay like that; I tried to be prepared, to know it wasn't over.

One night, I woke with relief from a sleep with no dreams. Michael slept beside me on one side. On the other side, the camera's tiny green light beamed stolidly in the darkness, faint but reassuring. My bladder was throbbing, and I dragged myself up and crossed the bedroom to the master bathroom that adjoined the room on Michael's side. I shut the door carefully, not wanting to disturb Michael's sleep, and turned on the light. I winced initially in the harsh white light, but by the time I was finished relieving myself, my eyes had adjusted.

Before returning to the bedroom, I began inspecting myself, beginning with my arms from wrist to shoulder, then my legs from ankle to thigh. No new marks. I faced the mirror and lifted my shirt to check my stomach and chest, even the folds under my breasts. Nothing. I pulled my shorts down and turned and stood on my tiptoes to check my buttocks, no longer feeling silly about doing it. It had become a ritual every time I woke up, as soon as I had a moment to myself, ever since the bite mark. My skin was clear. I swiveled slowly back to face myself in the mirror. I paused, staring into my own eyes. I put my hands on the edge of the counter and pressed down and leaned forward, pushing my face closer to the mirror.

My face was thin and pale. My eyes were puffy and there were dark circles beneath them. I thought maybe I could detect the beginnings of lines around my mouth, along the middle of my forehead, and at the corners of my eyes.

Is this aging? Or something else?

I pulled my hair back from my face on one side and studied my temples for gray, but couldn't find anything. My focus returned to my eyes, wide and unblinking.

I look . . . afraid. I wasn't sure when I started looking like that, or if I looked like that all the time. I wondered if other people could see it.

I tore my gaze from my reflection. I needed to go back to sleep. I reached for the doorknob with my right hand and the light switch with my left, then pulled the door open and simultaneously flipped the switch. At the same time, I saw it in the corner of the bedroom. In the brief moment of illumination before the room was plunged into darkness, I saw it standing in the corner across the room, lurking, hunched in the shadowy corner of the bedroom, immediately to the side of the camera and out of its sight, a fleshy humanoid form, staring at the spot where I laid my head every night. Waiting.

My finger never left the switch and I flipped it back on a split second later. Before I realized I was making it, a shriek had escaped my lips and I was shouting for Michael to wake up. If I had had time to think about it, maybe I would have realized that no one could have been there. That a man couldn't disappear that quickly. That there was nowhere it could have gone. But I did shout, and Michael flung his covers aside and sprang out of bed, looking around wildly and shouting, "What? What is it?"

I was staring wildly at the empty corner of the room while Michael rushed to me, and it all happened too quickly for me to tell myself not to shout, *it's in your head.* I stammered, tears forming in my eyes, pointing a trembling finger at the empty space.

"Jana, what? What happened? What is it?"

"I saw something." My voice sounded high and panicked. Hysterical.

"What did you see?"

"It was some kind of creature and it was standing in the corner of our room. Next to my side of the bed."

"A creature?" He stared blankly at the corner where I pointed, looking from it to me and back, nothing but uncertainty on his face.

Something in me broke, seeing that uncertainty, the doubt, no share in my fear. "Michael." My voice turned to pleading and I clutched his hands and brought them to my heart. "Michael, I need you to believe me. Nothing that's been happening is normal. Something is out there, something we don't understand. You know me, you know I am a rational person." I tried not to cry as I begged him to believe me, praying I wasn't wrong about his opinion of me.

"I'm sorry, honey, I want to believe you but I'm having a tough time understanding."

I knew then that I needed to tell him the truth about my mom too, that if I didn't he'd never trust me again.

"First, there's something I should have told you a long time ago," I said. Michael stiffened, and my voice trembled uncontrollably. My stomach rolled, terrified at how he would react. "My mom most likely had schizophrenia. On top of all her anxiety problems, and the agoraphobia. She wouldn't ever get diagnosed, but I've talked to Dr. Goulding about it, and it sounds pretty textbook."

Michael's face cleared a little, tense apprehension replaced with concern. He sat back down on the edge of the bed and pulled me down next to him. "Are you saying you think you're schizophrenic?" he asked.

"No," I answered quickly. "Dr. Goulding says no. But I was so afraid to tell you, afraid you'd think I'm crazy because I have like a ten percent higher chance of getting it, and if we have kids . . . " My voice broke and tears streamed down my face. "I'm so sorry I didn't tell you sooner."

"Tell me what? That our kids have a ten percent higher chance of schizophrenia than other kids? Or not even that, right? Since it's just a grandparent? This is something you've been worried about?"

"Well, yeah."

"Well, my family has a history of diabetes and heart failure. Come on, Jana, you know we could handle something like that if it happened. Our kids will have an amazing support system and resources your mom never had. They'll be fine."

The crushing tightness in my chest began to dissipate at his reaction. I'd carried that intense, heavy guilt with me almost our entire relationship, and in his eyes it was another little thing that didn't matter, that we'd deal with if it happened. My head was swimming, and I gave a tearful laugh. "I'm an idiot," I said.

"There's been something horrible happening and I haven't been able to be honest with you because I was so afraid you'd think I'm crazy. I wanted proof. But I can't wait anymore and I'm asking you to believe me."

He sobered and took my hand. "What is it?"

"This whole time, the nightmares and everything, I've tried to look at the most likely scenarios. I've tried to set aside my fear and to look logically at each thing that's happened. But at some point, I have had to face that something is out there. I need you to believe me, something is doing this to us."

"What, Jana, what could be doing this?"

"I don't understand it, I don't know what it is, but I'm telling you it's real. It is not in my head; I've seen it everywhere. On the trails when we hiked for your birthday, walking along the road in front of our house, sitting at your computer. It's talked to me in your voice, it's touched me with your hands. All those nights, it looked like you. One night, it sat on our bed and talked to me while you were sleeping behind me."

"What?" he interjected sharply. "Are you serious?"

"There is nothing we know in this world that could do the things it's done, but we're not so arrogant as to think we know everything in this world, are we? Please, you know I'm not the kind of person to think something like this easily. You know me."

He stared at me in silence while I spoke, squeezing my hands, trying to look reassuring and calm. When I finished, he held my eyes for a moment longer, a silent beat that seemed to hold my future in its hands, before opening his mouth and saying simply, "Okay. I believe you."

I issued a sharp exhale of relief and let my head fall against his chest. "Thank you."

Was it really so simple?

I wrapped my arms around him. He held me tightly, and I wondered if I had been my own worst enemy at every turn, telling him not to listen to me, telling him it was all in my head, discrediting myself. If I had demanded that he believe me earlier, everything could have been so much easier.

"You really believe me?" I asked.

"Jana, you're not wrong about being a rational person. I know you are. I know you've done everything you can to rule out other explanations. I know how hard it must have been for you to tell me something this wild. So, yeah. If you tell me something else is happening, I believe you. I don't understand what it is and I don't know what to do, but I believe you."

I had never loved him more than in that moment, and I believed for the first time in months that everything truly was going to be okay. We began to talk through everything. From the minor details I had left out when I would tell him I had a strange dream, to the dream about the thing in the forest, to the figure who sat next to me on the bed while Michael slept behind me. I told him everything. The only thing I still couldn't bring myself to tell him was the bite mark. I couldn't say why; a strange sense of shame and fear that it would upset him too much silenced me.

At the end, Michael ran his hands through his hair and pursed his lips. "Do you think it's our house?" he asked.

"No. We lived here for a year without anything happening."

"Maybe you should talk to Dr. Goulding?"

I glared at him. "Why would you say that?"

"I don't know, Jana. Just to cross everything off our list. Tell her everything you've seen and see if she still thinks it's nothing but waking nightmares. Maybe she'll even know of someone else we can talk to. Maybe she has other clients who have experienced things beyond her help."

"Okay," I said, working to keep my voice neutral. "I have my session tomorrow. I don't see why I can't go."

We talked for a little while longer before we laid back down, curled together in the center of our bed, safely in the circle of our camera's view. Michael fell asleep after a while, but I lay awake the rest of the night, my eyes fixed on the slow-blinking green light, and the dark space behind it.

CHAPTER THIRTY-ONE

I **CALLED IN** the next day. My therapy session was in the afternoon, and I had been planning to leave work early for it. I decided to take the day instead. I knew I wouldn't be able to focus anyway. *Just to cross everything off our list.* I wondered what Michael meant by that. I'd been so relieved that he accepted everything I said with minimal questioning, but I started wondering what it meant in his mind when he said he believed me. Maybe he was only trying to humor me and nudge me toward a diagnosis that would lead to more medication.

But I was nothing if not reasonable, I told myself. I would go to the session and I would talk to Dr. Goulding openly and honestly about the things I had seen, and if she told me I had schizophrenia . . .

"I saw something again," I said at the beginning of our session.

"What was it this time?"

"I was coming back from the bathroom in the middle of the night. Michael was asleep. For a split second, I saw a naked figure hunched in the corner of the bedroom, near the top of my side of the bed." *Just out of view of the camera,* I did not add, because that would imply that I thought there was something the camera would see, and maybe that would make me sound paranoid to her. Not a trait I wanted standing out right then.

"That sounds frightening," she said.

"It was."

"If it was, as you said, only for a split second, do you think you really saw it or was it something you imagined for a moment, like we all sometimes imagine we see things out of the corner of our eye?"

A flash of irritation moved through me at her comparison, implying that the thing I saw was nothing more than a shadow.

"I saw it," I said firmly.

"Then another waking nightmare," she said, sounding disappointed and almost let down. "Even though you've been taking the sleeping pills?"

Shit. I flushed with anger, realizing in that moment just how pointless it was that I was there. She would blame everything on my unwillingness to medicate and that was that. "I did stop taking them," I said unwillingly, forcing the words from my mouth with as much poise and self-assurance as I could muster.

I knew what she was going to say next, and she did. She launched into a defense of her recommendations and stressed the importance of following them, or at least being honest with her if I did not intend to follow them so she could work to offer alternate solutions.

Michael believes me. The refrain played in my head repeatedly as she spoke, reassuring myself that whatever Dr. Goulding thought didn't matter, and I hoped it was true. I left her office an hour later in relief. I tried to plan out what to tell Michael; if I told him Dr. Goulding said the same exact thing as before, maybe he would say it was reasonable for me to keep trying the sleeping pills. I hadn't told him about the bite mark, after all. He didn't know.

Everything about my position felt precarious.

Ivy. I had to tell Ivy. I had to try the same straightforward honesty I had tried with Michael; I had to see if she would believe me in the same way, only stronger—because everything Ivy did, she did with all of herself. It would be easier to tell her about the bite mark, too.

***

Ivy's bookshop was near Dr. Goulding's office, so I went straight there. I kept meeting my own eyes in my rearview mirror, wild and nervous, my face flushed. I was almost tingling with anxiety over telling her, but it was time. It was time to put it all out into the open and let everything fall where it would.

When I arrived at Ivy's bookshop and found it empty of customers, it seemed a sign in my favor.

"Jana." She sounded surprised and confused. "What's going on?"

"Ivy, I need to talk to you. This whole dream thing, it's more than that. Something strange is happening and I finally opened up to Michael about it and he believes me, and I need you to know about it, too." I flipped the sign on her front door without asking and sat down with her while she stared at me, wide-eyed.

"Okay, Jana, you're freaking me out a little, but tell me what's going on."

And I told her. I told her everything, including the bite mark this time, more openly and honestly than I had even with Michael, emboldened now and demanding in my determination to be taken seriously.

"Wow." It was all she said for a moment, once I finished, and I stared at her expectantly. "So, what do you think is after you?" she asked.

"I don't know," I said. "The thing that's been getting to me about it... This isn't some ghost or spirit. It's impersonating someone I love. What if there are beings out there, beyond some kind of wall that we can't see or touch . . . What if they can just look through, and see something they want . . . For their own amusement or pleasure. For fun. To *fuck* with me."

"Why would it happen all of the sudden?"

"I don't know," I said.

"Why doesn't it happen to other people?" Ivy asked.

"Maybe it does, maybe it happens all the time . . . " I said, but then my attention went back to her face, and I noticed the worried crinkle between her eyes. She wasn't asking questions in an effort to understand and help me solve the mystery; she was asking questions the way you ask questions to disprove someone when you don't want to outright tell them they're wrong. She was gently steering me, hoping I would talk myself out of it, as though she was worried I actually believed it.

"You don't believe me," I said flatly. "I honestly thought it would be easier to convince you than Michael, but he believed me with even less to go on. I didn't tell him all of it, but he still believed me." My voice was rising in anger now. "Because he knows me and loves me enough to know I am not a crazy person."

"Look, Jana," Ivy cut me off. "I wasn't supposed to tell you this. And I know it would be putting you in a bad position in your marriage if I asked you not to tell Michael I told you, so I won't bother. But I hope you won't be too mad at him. He loves you so damn much and I think he's genuinely trying to do everything he can to help."

"What?" It was like a gut punch. "What are you talking about?"

"He came by earlier. He wanted to warn me about . . . all this." She was trying to speak delicately and placed her hand over mine as she spoke. "He said he talked to Dr. Goulding about it and that we all needed to be on the same page about the fact that you need to be taking her advice. You have to listen to your therapist, Jana." She stared at me, all regret and sympathy.

My head spun. Everything I was afraid of happening, every worst-case scenario I had thought of, seemed to be coming true. Not only had Michael been lying about believing me to placate me, to placate a crazy woman, but he had also gone behind my back to make sure the only other person I trusted in the entire world wouldn't believe me, either.

"I have to go." I grabbed my things and turned, unable to meet her eyes.

Everyone playing along to keep the crazy lady calm.

"Jana, wait. Don't be mad. Nobody thinks anything bad about you! We just want to help."

I waved—a lump forming in my throat keeping me from talking even if I'd wanted to—and rushed out. I started the car and pulled away as quickly as I could, blinking away tears. My vision was blurred and I began driving without knowing where I would go, but I was unwilling to stay outside Ivy's bookshop a moment longer. I knew she would be close behind me.

***

Somehow, I ended up back at Dr. Goulding's office. I wasn't sure what I expected to accomplish, but one thing in particular that Ivy had said stood out to me—*he talked to Dr. Goulding about it.* It was an unacceptable betrayal. The number of things I knew for sure in the world seemed to be rapidly diminishing, but I knew about patient confidentiality.

How dare she?

She deserved to be confronted about it, and she owed me an explanation, and it would be easier to confront her than Michael. She had smiled into my face hours earlier and told me all my problems could be solved with a sleeping pill, while whispering behind my back that everyone I loved needed to be on the watch, that my mental state was slipping.

Her office was an independent practice and she was the only therapist. She occasionally took on university students who helped with office work, answered phones, and scheduled appointments, but when I returned to the office that afternoon, everyone had gone home. The front door was unlocked and I entered, but the front room was empty. The receptionist desk was abandoned, as it often was (*Just come straight into my office if the door is cracked or open and if it's closed give it a tap*—that's what Dr. Goulding had told me when I first started seeing her).

The door was cracked.

A small sense of foreboding began to prickle at the nape of my neck, but I couldn't have said why. The front room looked more like an eclectic, quirky living room, splashed in colorful throw pillows and handmade frames, than an office waiting room. Though the light was off, streams of diminishing sunlight filtered in through the cracked office door. I approached it slowly.

"Dr. Goulding?" I called. "It's Jana Brookes."

"Come on in." Her voice filled me with relief, and I moved forward with more confidence. I pressed the door open and saw her bent over paperwork at her desk.

"Jana, what are you doing back here? What can I help you with?" The blinds were open and let in the daylight, but the light was off in there as well. She didn't look up as she spoke.

"I just spoke with my sister," I began, "and she said you spoke with Michael about me." The words were out that quickly and I was finished. Such a simple, short statement, yet it seemed like it should be all that was needed. She was my therapist, and she had betrayed me.

Then she looked up. She met my eyes, and she smiled.

She was wrong, all wrong, worse than the time the awful caricature of Michael greeted me in his office. Like it didn't even put very much effort into replicating her.

"Do you think this begins and ends with Michael?" She leaned forward, her eyes mocking. "Or with you for that matter, Jana?"

I wanted to scream, but it was frozen in my throat. I stared at it, face-to-face in the light for the second time, and I couldn't move, couldn't think. After a couple crawling seconds passed, I swallowed hard, trying to muster enough moisture in my dry throat to speak. "Why are you doing this to me?" My voice was weak and scratchy.

Dr. Goulding's plasticky face assumed an expression of a long-suffering adult talking to a child. "Because it's easy," she said in her best therapist voice. "Poor Jana with her poor sick mother and all her fears and mistrust of her *own* mind. Why *wouldn't* I?"

I fled. I ran from the office, slamming the door behind me and not looking back until I got into my car, and I sped away.

Chapter Thirty-Two

I WAS RELIEVED to get home. I was angry and eager to confront Michael, and I blamed him for what I'd faced in Dr. Goulding's office. The thing wanted us against each other, I was sure of it now, and Michael's betrayal had played me right into its hands. I slammed my car door and marched into the house and straight up the stairs, knowing I would find him in his office.

"How could you?" I flew into the room in a flurry, slamming that door too. Holly jumped to her feet beside Michael.

He looked up, startled. "What?"

"You went behind my back! You turned Ivy against me, and you talked to my fucking therapist? You're . . . you're . . . " I sputtered, searching for the word. "You're gaslighting me! I cannot believe you would do that to me!"

His eyes opened wide and he stared at me. "Jana." His voice was low and cautious. And . . . afraid? Why would Michael look afraid? "What happened?" he asked.

I stood where I was and we stared at each other across the room, adversaries or partners, foes or allies, and I didn't know which. I chose my words carefully and spoke evenly. "I saw Ivy today. She said you went by her shop and talked to her about me. She made it sound like you told her not to listen to me. Like I'm going crazy."

"Jana . . . I have never once in my life been to Ivy's shop without you."

The words fell between us and hung there, changing everything. Terrified that it would be another thing he doubted, another argument caused by indiscretions he thought were all in my head, I pulled my phone out and opened Ivy's conversation history. Though I had ignored every message and call, she had sent several.

Jana, sorry if you feel betrayed. We're trying to help.
Please don't be mad at Michael.
If your therapist is talking to Michael, there has to be a reason.
You ARE smart enough to know that.

The look on Michael's face as he read those messages was one I had not seen before. For the first time, there was real terror in his eyes. He had stood and met me halfway across the room when I handed him my phone, and now he felt for his chair behind him and collapsed back into it.

"I've never talked to Ivy about you," he whispered, hushed like he was afraid someone was listening.

"I'm so glad. Oh god, Michael, it's been pitting us against each other." I dropped to my knees and put my head in his lap, and he ran his hand through my hair. "Now you see," I said. "Now you really believe me."

"Yes." His hand was trembling. "I'm so sorry."

"It's okay."

Michael was grappling with his first real introduction to the fear I'd been carrying for months, and I knew in that moment that when he said he believed me the night before, he didn't know what he was agreeing to believe, he only knew he wanted to believe me. Meanwhile, a giddy thrill shot through me and I tried to suppress the grin that threatened to split across my face, because I saw what this latest ruse really meant.

It was caught.

It had overplayed, it had gone too far.

Now I had more proof than I ever needed. The moment I got Ivy in a room with Michael, he would tell her it wasn't him she talked to, and then she would know. And with both of them on my side, it felt like anything was possible, like maybe we could find a way to escape this thing.

"We have to have Ivy come over and explain what happened," I said. "We'll do it tomorrow."

"Okay. What do we do after that?"

"I don't know yet."

His eyes were darting incessantly around the room and fixating on the door, as though at any moment he expected something to come through, and I shuddered.

"Do you want to watch television in bed and talk through everything more?" I asked. The bed seemed like the safest place somehow, a constantly monitored zone that hadn't been violated since the camera was set up. He nodded numbly and we moved downstairs, Holly close behind us. She hesitated at the doorway, normally off limits, but Michael waved her in. We didn't think twice about breaking the rule that night. She bounded into the room and leapt onto the bed, turning around several times while Michael's eyes followed her, both dazed and amused. She finally curled up at the foot of our bed like it was where she'd always belonged.

"I'm going to go shower," I said. I was sweaty and drained.

"Okay." Michael sat gingerly on the edge of the bed and rested a hand on Holly like a lifeline. She seemed to steady him. "I'm going to . . . I dunno, research priests or something, I guess."

I offered a wan smile and went to the bathroom. I stayed in the shower a long time, thinking over everything, alternating between the most profound relief I'd ever felt in my life, relief that the first phase of my plan was accomplished, and terror over not knowing what needed to come next, not having a second phase.

When I finished, I returned to the bedroom to see Michael still lying in bed where I'd left him. He offered a comforting smile, calmer now, and I smiled back. We were in it together. I crawled into the bed and pressed against him, his body perfectly filling in the spaces of mine; his leg tucked between mine, one arm wrapped around me, my head on his chest. I breathed in deeply, content.

"I love you," I told him suddenly. We always said it often, casually, but my voice was somber in that moment. He had been there for me while I felt like my mind was slipping away from me, and he remained there when even I didn't trust myself. And now he was there still, ready to face whatever darkness was tormenting me, together. I was suddenly desperate for him to know how much he meant to me.

"I love you, too," he answered. He said it readily and sincerely, but I stiffened involuntarily. Something in his voice.

Unable to keep the nervous quiver from my voice, I asked, "Michael?"

A small, concerned crinkle appeared between his eyebrows. His eyes stared into mine; patient, inquisitive, amused.

"No."

Cold dread spread through my limbs. Blood rushed to my head and pounded in my ears, drowning out the thudding of my heart.

I laughed weakly, suddenly aware of the smallness of the bedroom, the abandoned space at the foot of the bed, the closed door behind me, the silence of the rest of the house.

He looked perfect now. He sounded perfect. Believable in every way. Except that he didn't care if I believed it anymore. Maybe that was part of the game.

In my exhaustion and hopelessness, a terrible resignation filled me. I imagined tearing myself away from him and running out of the bedroom. I imagined him staying motionless at first, staring after me with that small smile on his face, calm and innocently puzzled. I imagined running into the street, asking for help, trying to explain that my husband wasn't my husband.

All while he stood beside me, concerned and loving, even apologetic, barely having to defend himself from something so ludicrous. Even Ivy would look on with sympathy for him in all he was being forced to deal with.

Maybe that's how it would go. Or maybe I would never even make it past the door.

My next question required more courage than anything I had ever done in my life. Part of me knew that acknowledging it, that pulling down the facade I hated so much but was terrified to remove, would lead to more terrible things than anything I had experienced. But I had to know.

"Is he safe?" My voice was small, and I couldn't lift my eyes to his.

He softly smoothed my hair and brushed a strand from my face, arranging it carefully. I struggled not to shudder in revulsion as the arm that was tucked behind me snaked further around to encircle my waist, and his lips brushed the top of my head.

"As long as you're good."

Six feet is not deep enough in this Mystery Thriller...

Come listen when the Dead speak...

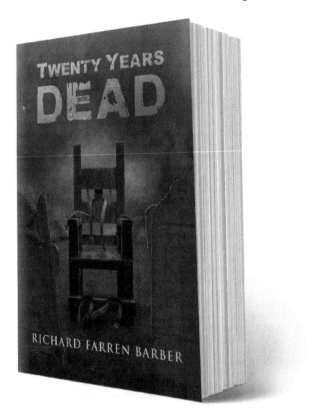

THE END?

Not if you want to dive into more of Crystal Lake Publishing's Tales from the Darkest Depths!

Check out our amazing website and online store.
https://www.crystallakepub.com

We always have great new projects and content on the website to dive into, as well as a newsletter, behind the scenes options, social media platforms, our own dark fiction shared-world series and our very own webstore. If you use the IGotMyCLPBook! coupon code in the store (at the checkout), you'll get a one-time-only 50% discount on your first eBook purchase!

Our webstore even has categories specifically for KU books, non-fiction, anthologies, and of course more novels and novellas.

ACKNOWLEDGEMENTS

Thank you to everyone who read this book in its earliest stages and offered encouragement along the way—Lydia, who believed in this book more than I did and has read it nearly as many times; Eric, who was there for me through every moment of this story's creation; Finley, the most patient and insightful critique partner I could ask for; and Rachael, who doesn't like horror but will always read mine. Thanks also to Dr. Jeremy Vincent for his insight as a psychologist. My family and friends who have supported me in countless ways, I appreciate you all so much and would not have gotten here without you.

About the Author

Faith Pierce writes horror, dark fantasy, and other forms of speculative fiction. Her short stories have been published with The NoSleep Podcast, Cemetery Gates, Kandisha Press, and Scare Street. Her debut novel is planned for release with Crystal Lake Publishing in 2022.

Faith grew up in a small town in Texas and currently lives in Missouri with her son and their dog.

It's not that there aren't good people in the world. It's that the bad ones are so much easier to find.

Readers . . .

Thank you for reading *The Face You Wear*. We hope you enjoyed this novel.

If you have a moment, please review *The Face You Wear* at the store where you bought it.

Help other readers by telling them why you enjoyed this book. No need to write an in-depth discussion. Even a single sentence will be greatly appreciated. Reviews go a long way to helping a book sell, and is great for an author's career. It'll also help us to continue publishing quality books. You can also share a photo of yourself holding this book with the hashtag #IGotMyCLPBook!

Thank you again for taking the time to journey with Crystal Lake Publishing.

Visit our Linktree page for a list of our social media platforms.
https://linktr.ee/CrystalLakePublishing

Our Mission Statement:

Since its founding in August 2012, Crystal Lake Publishing has quickly become one of the world's leading publishers of Dark Fiction and Horror books in print, eBook, and audio formats.

While we strive to present only the highest quality fiction and entertainment, we also endeavour to support authors along their writing journey. We offer our time and experience in non-fiction projects, as well as author mentoring and services, at competitive prices.

With several Bram Stoker Award wins and many other wins and nominations (including the HWA's Specialty Press Award), Crystal Lake Publishing puts integrity, honor, and respect at the forefront of our publishing operations.

We strive for each book and outreach program we spearhead to not only entertain and touch or comment on issues that affect our readers, but also to strengthen and support the Dark Fiction field and its authors.

Not only do we find and publish authors we believe are destined for greatness, but we strive to work with men and woman who endeavour to be decent human beings who care more for others than themselves, while still being hard working, driven, and passionate artists and storytellers.

Crystal Lake Publishing is and will always be a beacon of what passion and dedication, combined with overwhelming teamwork and respect, can accomplish. We endeavour to know each and every one of our readers, while building personal relationships with our authors, reviewers, bloggers, podcasters, bookstores, and libraries.

We will be as trustworthy, forthright, and transparent as any business can be, while also keeping most of the headaches away from our authors, since it's our job to solve the problems so they can stay in a creative mind. Which of course also means paying our authors.

We do not just publish books, we present to you worlds within your world, doors within your mind, from talented authors who sacrifice so much for a moment of your time.

There are some amazing small presses out there, and through collaboration and open forums we will continue to support other presses in the goal of helping authors and showing the world what quality small presses are capable of accomplishing. No one wins when a small press goes down, so we will always be there to support hardworking, legitimate presses and their authors. We don't see Crystal Lake as the best press out there, but we will always strive to be the best, strive to be the most interactive and grateful, and even blessed press around. No matter what happens over time, we will also take our mission very seriously while appreciating where we are and enjoying the journey.

What do we offer our authors that they can't do for themselves through self-publishing?

We are big supporters of self-publishing (especially hybrid publishing), if done with care, patience, and planning. However, not every author has the time or inclination to do market research, advertise, and set up book launch strategies. Although a lot of authors are successful in doing it all, strong small presses will always be there for the authors who just want to do what they do best: write.

What we offer is experience, industry knowledge, contacts and trust built up over years. And due to our strong brand and trusting fanbase, every Crystal Lake Publishing book comes with weight of respect. In time our fans begin to trust our judgment and will try a new author purely based on our support of said author.

With each launch we strive to fine-tune our approach, learn from our mistakes, and increase our reach. We continue to assure our authors that we're here for them and that we'll carry the weight of the launch and dealing with third parties while they focus on their strengths—be it writing, interviews, blogs, signings, etc.

We also offer several mentoring packages to authors that include knowledge and skills they can use in both traditional and self-publishing endeavours.

We look forward to launching many new careers.

This is what we believe in. What we stand for. This will be our legacy.

Welcome to Crystal Lake Publishing—
Tales from the Darkest Depths.

Made in the USA
Middletown, DE
12 August 2022

71270342R00113